I HOLD A WOLF BY THE EARS

I HOLD A WOL

FARRAR, STRAUS AND GIROUX   NEW YORK

Y THE EARS STORIES

LAURA VAN DEN BERG

Farrar, Straus and Giroux
120 Broadway, New York 10271

Printed in the United States of America
First edition, 2020

Interior photograph by leedsn / Shutterstock.com

Library of Congress Cataloging-in-Publication Data
Names: Van den Berg, Laura, author.
Title: I hold a wolf by the ears : stories / Laura van den Berg.
Description: First edition. | New York : Farrar, Straus and Giroux, 2020.
Identifiers: LCCN 2020003450 | ISBN 9780374102098 (hardcover)
Classification: LCC PS3622.A58537 A6 2020 | DDC 813/.6—dc23
LC record available at https://lccn.loc.gov/2020003450

Designed by Abby Kagan

Our books may be purchased in bulk for promotional, educational, or business
use. Please contact your local bookseller or the Macmillan Corporate and
Premium Sales Department at 1-800-221-7945, extension 5442, or by e-mail at
MacmillanSpecialMarkets@macmillan.com.

www.fsgbooks.com
www.twitter.com/fsgbooks • www.facebook.com/fsgbooks

10 9 8 7 6 5 4 3 2 1

TO EMILY AND KATHERINE
two of the fiercest women I know

TO MY DAD
you are missed

Do you ever suddenly find it strange to be yourself?

—CLARICE LISPECTOR

CONTENTS

LAST NIGHT

want to tell you about the night I got hit by a train and died.

The thing is—it never happened.

This was many years ago.

I didn't think about that night, my last night, for a long time and then one day I woke up and it was all I could think about.

Let me try to explain. I've spent years cultivating a noisy life. I live in a city riddled with unending construction projects, in an apartment above a bar. I see student after student during office hours; I let their words replace my thoughts. I volunteer at a women's crisis center in my neighborhood. I listen to the women tell me what's happened to their lives. Recently, though, silence has snuck in. For one thing, the bar closed the day after Thanksgiving without any warning at all, casting the whole block in quiet.

I blame that shuttered bar for the return of my last night.

I was seventeen and I had been in this place for ten months, receiving treatment for my various attempts to kill myself. My parents had mortgaged their house to keep me there and it was only in my last two months that I agreed to talk to them on the phone and even then it was mostly out of boredom. I was that angry they wanted me to live.

This place was in a rural pocket of central Florida and they had kept me too long. I knew because by the time they got around to discharging me, I had forgotten how to shave my legs. I had forgotten about the existence of mouthwash (alcohol) and dental floss (hanging). I had forgotten the sound of the ocean. I had forgotten about cable TV and the Internet. I had forgotten the other world.

My fellow patients had started speaking to me the way I imagined they might to someone soon departing on a dangerous and unknowable mission. A skittish hand on my shoulder, followed by *Stay safe* or *Good luck out there* or *I hope I never see you again.*

On my last night, I could not sleep. I was terrified. This place had kept me alive for the last ten months and soon it would be up to me. The other two girls in my room couldn't sleep either. The three of us, we had become something like friends.

"It's your last night," they agreed. "We should do something."

At midnight, or at an hour I remember to be midnight, we found the orderly, a white guy who always wore a baseball cap indoors. Million-dollar smile. We asked him to let us outside.

"It's her last night," the two roommates pleaded, trying their best to look harmless. This facility specialized in the mental troubles of women and we were among the youngest patients, which made us feel superior. We had our whole lives in front of us—*maybe*. If we chose to. What power!

"All we want is to take a walk," I said. "Down the road and back."

When I asked the question, I was banking on one of two outcomes: an unmovable *no* or a trade, because this orderly had always struck me as the type. In the lull before he answered, I calculated what I was willing to offer.

A hand job, for example, I could do in my sleep.

Because we wanted that warm midnight air.

Because I felt it would be my responsibility, given that this was my last night.

"Goodbye, kid," the orderly said. "Hurry back."

"What?" I'd never heard him call anyone *kid* before.

"Those were Humphrey Bogart's last words," he told us. "All the way back in 1957. Don't ever forget: Humphrey Bogart was a juvenile delinquent who went on to do great things."

And then he let us go! I still can't believe it. If one of my students wrote that in a story I would call instant bullshit. Why would he risk his job? Why was he the *only* orderly on overnight in the first place? I would interrogate this imaginary student, all the while thinking *You don't know what the fuck you're talking about*, and I would be so wrong—because it really did happen like that, he really did let us go, and this is the problem with translating experience into fiction, the way certain truths read like lies.

Maybe he thought I had too much to lose, since it was my last night.

Maybe he knew we were in the middle of nowhere and had no place to go.

Maybe he knew every morning I stared up at the white ceiling as I swallowed my meds and thought, *You've won.* Because that's when they let you go—not when you were well, but when you gave up the fight.

I wonder if this orderly still works as an orderly.

I wonder if he's still alive.

I can't remember his name or see his face, just the brim of his baseball cap shadowing his eyes and that million-dollar smile.

About the place itself I remember every detail. Even today, from the quiet bewilderment of middle age, I could draw it all from memory. They had gone for a "homey" look, which meant floral curtains with scalloped edges were pulled closed over every window, to cover the bars. The curtains were cheap, so during a sunlit day we could see the bars through the fabric, solid as trees.

The three of us slipped out a back door and started walking down a dirt road, in the direction of the train tracks, and here is the part about which I am most ashamed. We lived together for ten months, me and these two girls. We sat together at meals. We sat together on movie night. An island of girl. We brushed each other's hair. We pinched each other's waists. We touched each other's lips. Bellies. Wet insides of mouths. We wept secrets. We eavesdropped nightmares. We conspired about how to ditch or switch our meds, back when we still had the will (I arrived addicted to prescription drugs, and coveted one roommate's Klonopin).

Yet—

I could not tell you their names. I have forgotten them. Their faces are twin black holes, deep space. I remember more about that stupid orderly, the way his baseball cap looked like it had been molded onto his head. What kind of person could forget?

Around the holidays, the women's crisis center brings in a counselor who has agreed to donate sessions to the volunteers; this is their gift to us. On Monday and Friday afternoons, the counselor sits in the art room upstairs. None of the other volunteers go to see her, so I do and when the free counselor says that she can tell I'm resilient, that I do what it takes, I try to not hear this as an accusation.

As it turned out, I was too ambitious to be a permanent drug addict. I had plans and drinking seemed more compatible with plans, but that was exactly what compelled me to climb the creaky stairs to the art room in the first place—one too many hangovers. I tell the free counselor that I want a sober way to exist outside time and she suggests I take up swimming. Five mornings a week, I wake before dawn and trek to an indoor pool. I swim until I can't lift my arms, until I'm so weak I could drown. When the free counselor asks me if swimming makes me feel good, I tell her it makes me feel obliterated. By the time I leave the pool, I can scarcely remember what day it is or if I already ate breakfast. Everything I own smells of chlorine.

"It's working," I insist in the art room.

Here is what passed for therapy in Florida, all those years ago: once a month a local hypnotist would come up from Sarasota to help us uncover our buried and traumatic memories. She wore an excessive amount of jade. Most of my fellow patients did have traumatic memories that were very much unburied, the kinds of stories that would make people in the outside world cluck and whisper, *Can you imagine?* Still, this hypnotist persisted in her digging.

Not me, though. I had nothing to give her.

The hypnotist disagreed.

The first time we met, she took my hands, the silver bands of her rings cold on my skin, and told me she believed with all her heart that something unspeakably awful had happened to me and that my memory had concealed this awfulness, in an attempt to save my life, and that this unprocessed trauma was the source of all my troubles.

After she said this, I refused to go under hypnosis. My commitment to the truth simply did not run that deep. I thought she looked like a fraud too, weighed down by all that jade.

Her monthly visits were a worrisome time at the facility. The woman with the worst story wouldn't eat or speak for several days afterward. I tried to tell the others about my refusal, as this place could make us do a great many things yet they could only exert so much control over our unconscious minds, but everyone else wanted to keep getting hypnotized and letting her dig around and so what more could I do.

Most of us had been sent here by our loved ones and hated them for it, but the woman with the worst story had sent herself here, emptied her own savings, mortgaged her own house. She had the worst story and still she wanted that badly to live.

When I tell the free counselor about the hypnosis, she is appalled.

"Amateurs," she says.

I add that the hypnotist might have been an amateur and a fraud, but nevertheless her words have haunted me ever since.

After these sessions in the art room, I walk neighborhoods I do not live in and snap photos like a tourist. A strange shadow cast in a park. Window boxes packed with ice and dirt, empty of flowers. On the way home, while waiting on the T platform, I take care to stand a healthy distance from the tracks, my back pressed to the tiled wall.

You notice details, you write them down. You cultivate your eye. This, I tell my students, is what a writer does.

About these two girls the only details I can salvage are a few facts from their stories.

One had been institutionalized twice before. All the treatments, all the attempts to save her life, had bankrupted her family—her parents, her fiancé; her fiancé's family was even in danger. On her first night, she said, "I keep trying to tell them that it would be the greatest kindness to just let me die."

The other one had been raped by her older brother. For years.

Her brother was the only person who ever sent her mail. Short, handwritten letters that focused on the weather.

I hope these girls have forgotten me just as completely. I hope they remember only a single humiliating, dehumanizing detail. That would be equitable, at least. Assuming they are still alive.

On our last night, the dust from the road made the air look fogged.

I am telling a story now.

The train tracks were elevated. We scrambled up a scrubby rise and balanced on the steel edges, dazed by our sudden freedom. We could barely make out the facility lights through the thin trees; that world, which had become *the* world, felt very far away. We did not talk about how tomorrow I would be gone, vanished before breakfast.

"What's the first thing you're going to do?" the facility director had asked me that afternoon, in our final session. This man was in his early fifties. He wore flip-flops to work. Sunglasses hung from a lanyard around his tan neck. Divorced but still a pale band where his wedding ring used to be. On Sundays, he drove a van into the nearest town for a supervised lunch at Olive Garden, where we, all adult or near-adult women, made obscene gestures with breadsticks and he, the facility director, was powerless to stop us.

The night air was still and heavy. It made me think of blood.

"A lot of people commit suicide by train," said the roommate who had been institutionalized twice before. "Thousands of people in North America alone."

Years later—I will read a novel where the protagonist's sister commits suicide by train and cry for days. I will attempt to have a conversation with an acquaintance about the book and this person will fall under the impression that I, so overcome, must have lost a sibling to suicide and I will not be able to stop crying long enough to explain otherwise.

Later still—at the crisis center, I will take a workshop on speaking to people exhibiting suicidal ideation, for the volunteers who answer the helpline. The workshop leader will discuss the movement to change the language from *committed suicide* to *died by suicide*, since *commit* implies acting with intent and a person whose life ends in suicide is, we can only assume, too distressed to intend anything.

The problem with the helpline is that most people are calling about things no one can help them with.

Everyone else is calling about a parking pass.

They want to come in for a free meal or to use the computers and know the neighborhood is impossible to park in. Or they want to donate old clothes, books.

The workshop leader will suggest we focus on forward-thinking, open-ended questions. "What's one small thing you could do today to better your life?" I will ask a woman who calls the helpline one afternoon, picking from a list the workshop leader provided. "If I could answer that question do you really think I'd be calling this stupid number?" the woman will say back.

I wish the workshop leader could have met the roommate who knew so much about suicide by train. She's coming back to me now, this girl—very tall, her dark hair long and straight as a curtain. I remember the way she spoke lovingly about all her attempts, like a career criminal reviewing past and future heists—her plans, what went wrong at the last moment, what she would do differently next time, one last big job and then she's out.

I have never met a person so clear.

I remember being very impressed that she had acquired a fiancé. He sent one postcard a week, called every Sunday.

None of us knew if the train tracks were still in use or abandoned. We assumed they were derelict, since we could not ever remember hearing a train whistle. I pointed out that it would be awfully risky, working train tracks down the road from a facility for mentally disturbed women.

The second roommate, the one with the perverted brother, was a redhead with translucent eyelashes.

She said, "I hear a train coming."

"Shut the fuck up," the tall roommate said. "You don't either." She was always telling people to *shut the fuck up*. It was a term of endearment.

"I do too," said the redhead.

I imagined the ground shaking under my feet.

"People who commit suicide by train look like they're praying," said the tall one. "The way they kneel down and lay their heads on the tracks."

"What would you do on your last night?" The redhead turned to me. Her round pale face shimmered like a moon. "Would you pray?"

As it happened, I had recently started to pray—a fleeting thought shoved out into the ether before bed, a raft on a turbulent sea. I wondered if God found people like me annoying, those who turned to prayer only when they were neck-deep, that terrible friend we've all had.

"All I want right now is a cigarette," I said on the tracks. "After that, I don't know."

The next morning, at the airport, I will buy a pack and smoke the whole thing on the curb. I will get so sick, spend so much time puking and then dry heaving, my arms hugging the cold bowl, I will nearly miss my flight. On the plane, I will sob like I just left the love of my life behind.

"What I wouldn't give for a train." The tall roommate stared dreamily down the dark tracks.

The redhead jabbed two fingers in her mouth and made a shrill whistle.

"Stop that." I smacked at her hand. I didn't like how she was acting.

The redhead stuck her fingers back in her mouth and did it again.

"Oh, oh. Don't stop." The tall roommate slid a hand between her legs. "You're making me wet." That was what she said whenever she liked something, whenever she thought something was good—*you're making me wet.*

The more the redhead kept whistling, her two fingers buried in her mouth like a prong in a socket, the more I could see it. Hear it. Feel it. The palm fronds trembled. The tracks shuddered. I felt sweat on my rib cage. The bottoms of my laceless sneakers heated up.

A train was coming.

We were all still young enough that our deaths would be considered tragic, though the tall roommate was always telling us we owed it to ourselves to commit suicide before we had been ravaged by time. *Think of Alice*, she would implore, referring to the sixty-year-old who had been shipped to this place by her adult children after attempting to gas herself in her garage. Alice walked around with stains on her sweatpants and a sad bowl haircut and ingrown toenails. Alice had done electroshock in her thirties. *Think of Alice if you want to talk about what's tragic.*

When the New Year arrives, and it is almost here, I will be closer in age to Alice than to the girl who stood on those tracks, on her last night, thinking about trains.

Not long after that girl rejoined the world, she came to the conclusion that the self who spent ten months staring at bars through floral curtains must be killed, so the person the girl needed to become could take her place. It was a good plan, except she has proven resilient, that old self. Never more so than now.

I want to tell you about the night I got hit by a train and died.

The thing is—it never happened.

Because there was no train. Of course. We talked for a while—about what I can't remember—and tried to find stars we could name. We didn't know the name for anything except the Milky Way; we knew so little back then, the three of us. We returned at the appointed time. We knocked once and the orderly let us back in, flashed that million-dollar smile, confident in our dumb obedience. We crept into our room and got into our beds. Lights out. I slipped away on the edge of dawn. I have never traveled with so little. If they were awake they didn't say anything. Apparently we had all decided, without discussion, that we didn't believe in goodbyes.

This was a long time ago.

Long enough that it has ceased to feel like the defining period of my life.

Except sometimes.

Like when I see a train.

The weird thing is: I love trains. I never get tired of riding them.

After the free counselor's last day in the art room, I take the long way to the pool. It's still winter, the downstairs bar is still stuck in its sudden silence, though right now it's warm enough that I do not need to zip my coat. I wonder, as I have before, what would have happened if there really had been a train. If the tall roommate would have wanted to pray. If the redhead and I could have talked her down. *What's one small thing you could do today to better your life?* If the redhead would have seen her brother's face in ours and sent us flying. If we all would have come to our senses and gotten the fuck out of there. Or if I would have abandoned them both to the tracks, those ghosts I killed to survive.

SLUMBERLAND

spent that summer driving around at night and taking photographs because I could not stand the sound of my neighbor wailing through the walls. This neighbor lived in the apartment above me and when I passed her in the stairwells she looked perfectly regular, but at around ten o'clock at night she would start carrying on and her uncorked sadness had a physical effect on me: my skin itched, my teeth ached, a clear liquid leaked from one of my ears. Once I even got a nosebleed. I wondered if our other neighbors could hear her and if anyone had knocked on her door or called building management to complain. I did not knock on her door or call building management to complain because I did not want to confront whatever was happening in my neighbor's apartment; I wanted only to get away.

The apartment complex I was fleeing was north of Orlando, situated between the Deltona Lakes and the Seminole State Forest. My life there seemed provisional, even though I had no immediate plans to move, and so it felt natural to wander.

As I drove around looking for things to photograph, I added up what little I knew about my neighbor. She had lived in the apartment complex for six months. I did not know her first name, but from the mailboxes I knew her last (Novak). Unless that name was left over from the people who had lived there before, which was possible. Until this wailing situation I had not paid particularly close attention to the mailboxes. My neighbor had a shoulder tattoo that spelled out something inscrutable in dainty cursive lettering. I often passed her hauling swollen bags from Dollar Tree up and down the stairwell. I had no idea what she did for a living. We had never really spoken, just waves and nods. She used to have a cat, but a few months after she moved in the cat vanished. I remembered seeing signs in the laundry room: a photo of a black-and-white cat, the offer of a meager reward.

Things my neighbor did not know about me: I have taken photographs all my life. My first camera was a Kodak. I used to make my living as a wedding photographer, but after moving into the apartment complex I migrated over to pet portraiture. There was a surprising amount of money to be made in photographing German shepherds in bow ties. Plus no one ruins their life by getting a dog.

When I ran out of facts about my neighbor, I cataloged the subjects I had photographed so far: a sinkhole; roadkill; the molten night air and all the near-invisible things floating through it; the sidewalks still damp from afternoon rains; the long dark arcs of highways; fluorescent-lit parking lots; malls. There was a specific and terrible sadness to the malls, those places where people went to give in to their loneliness.

Sometimes I photographed human beings: a man sleeping under the scant shelter of a bus stop, a waitress smoking a cigarette outside an IHOP. Sometimes I parked in an unfamiliar neighborhood and walked around with my camera, my armpits dripping under my shirt. That was how I got the mother and son, haloed in the warm light of their kitchen. The mother was kneeling in front of her son, who looked to be about six or seven, and dabbing ointment on his forehead with her pinkie finger. So precise. So tender. Their house didn't have front lights or a fence and so to get this shot I crept onto their lawn, moving in a squat like the creature of the night I was becoming, ashamed of how much I enjoyed it.

If apprehended by the mother, I could have said—*I had what you had once, or a version of it, and I long to visit that lost world.*

When my phone buzzed at odd hours, I knew it was my sister, sending me WhatsApp messages from Kyrgyzstan, where she lived with her girlfriend because they were both in the Peace Corps. *How are you?* she would ask and I would feel the weight of all her unspoken questions, the questions she probably discussed with her girlfriend late at night. *Nearly ready for bed*, I would message back while stopped at a red light.

If my phone buzzed and it wasn't my sister then it was WhatsApp sending me strange spam messages, people asking for prayers or money or both. That summer, I got the same message—*pray that we get the duplex*—so frequently that every time I drove past a duplex I started thinking of the sender, whoever they were.

Parking and walking was also how I started photographing Slumberland, a motel at the end of a residential street, in my old neighborhood near Lake Monroe, an area I had not been back to in some time. The lodgers, mostly women checked in for extended stays, tended to look either like they had just arrived on earth or like they had been stuck in this motel for all eternity. Back when I lived in the neighborhood, every week it seemed some distraught woman was standing on the pitched roof and threatening to jump. This would set off a predictable series of events: Someone would alert the manager, who would stand out on the sidewalk, in front of the three-story Craftsman with a wild yard and a drooping porch. He would light a cigarette and gaze up at the woman with utter boredom and say, "Go right on ahead. It won't kill you." After that, he would go back inside and the woman would stand very still, looking a little stunned, and then scramble up the roof and through the third-floor attic window, which was how they always got up there in the first place, all of them agile as cats. I used to think that this manager had missed his true calling as a hostage negotiator.

Whenever I ended up at Slumberland, I checked to see if there was a woman on the roof. Then I photographed the old-fashioned neon sign, the name spelled out in cursive lettering, like my neighbor's tattoo, and the black cat that hunted lizards in the ferns by the entrance. I crept around the building to see if anyone had left the blinds open on the ground floor and if so what was happening in those rooms. Once I got a woman trimming her bangs with nail scissors.

Sometimes I had the feeling that someone was creeping up behind me—even though it was usually me who was creeping up behind someone. Moments when I would feel the air thicken all around and the hairs on the back of my neck would rise up like antennae. Yet when I spun around to look I would find only a half-lit sidewalk, an empty car, silence.

Across the street from Slumberland stood a sprawling white Victorian on a double lot, sunk deep in the rot of foreclosure. Every time I saw the house, and the long shadows it cast, I thought of my sister. Before she and her girlfriend joined the Peace Corps they worked for a foreclosure clean-out service; in fact, that was how they met. They had woeful stories about finding oxygen tanks and toilet chairs and sinister doll collections.

The wreckage of wrecked lives. Then there was what the banks covered up—that the house had been used as a brothel, with soiled mattresses in all the rooms and in the basement and so many discarded condoms on the floors my sister and her girl-friend had to use rakes. Or: a meth lab. Then there was what the owners did to take their revenge: menacing graffiti on the walls and cement in the plumbing and poisoned pets. That side of real estate, my sister and her girlfriend eventually decided, was a cycle of violence with no end.

One night, when I was prowling around Slumberland with my camera, I caught movement over there, two slim shadows slipping through the larger shadow of the foreclosed Victorian. I darted across the still street and snuck around the back, where I observed the cutting beam of a flashlight and two teenagers, a boy and a girl, pressing each other down into the grass. The light disappeared, one of them must have switched it off, but it was a clear night and in the moonlight I watched as they shed their clothes effortlessly, like dogs shaking off water. Their faces came together and then their bodies and that was when I started tak-ing photos. Later, when I clicked through the images in my parked car—the windows rolled tight and fogged, the radio at blast, my heart hammering—the teenagers looked like quicksil-ver spilled in the grass.

Was it better to die with a pillow under your head or stretched out in the grass?

That was the kind of question that could preoccupy me all night, the kind that caused my sister and her girlfriend to worry, because he had not died with a pillow under his head, he had died stretched out in the grass.

A dare, a climb, a fall.

That border between magic and annihilation crossed.

These photographs are my best work and no one will ever see them.

On the night in question, the shadows around the foreclosed house were quiet and there were no women on the roof, but there was a commotion coming from the third floor. The window to the attic bedroom was open, the walls bleached by a harsh light. I watched from the sidewalk, partially shielded by an oak tree. Two women were having an argument. About what I couldn't tell. And then a woman was scrambling out the window and onto the pitched roof. She stood, her bare feet spread for balance, and waved an object over her head, something small and hard and bright yellow, a drop of sunshine in her hand.

The woman on the roof wore a pink cotton nightgown that hit her knees. Her legs looked as sturdy as logs. Her hair, twisted up in a bun, sat like a nest on top of her head.

"Do you promise?" she kept shouting on the roof, dangling the object over the ledge. "Do you swear?"

The one inside must have promised, must have sworn, because the woman on the roof straightened her shoulders and nodded and then began her careful trek back inside. She was passing the hard yellow thing through the window when she slipped. Her hands slapped at the edges of the sill; the object clattered down the slope and fell to the sidewalk, smashed to pieces. The woman was beached on her stomach, her pink nightgown hiked up to her ass. "I'm sorry," she cried. "I'm so sorry."

I hoped the manager might come out and be moved to help. Maybe all this time he'd had a mattress stashed in his office, just in case. Because while it was unlikely that the fall would kill this woman, angles, I knew all too well, could be unpredictable and cruel.

"Don't let her fall," I whispered to the one inside, fingers hot and tight around my camera.

Two long arms shot out of the window and grabbed the flailing woman by her wrists. The one inside pulled; the one outside squirmed and kicked. With my camera I got her pointed feet just before she disappeared through the window, two pale fish arcing out of the sea.

The object she had been ransoming was a ceramic bird. It lay on the sidewalk with its head cracked open, its wings yellow splinters. The two little black feet were still intact, pointing in opposite directions.

East, west.

Left, right.

Clearly the bird had meant a lot to the woman inside, for reasons I would never know. Now a chunk of her private world was out here on display, for all to see and for no one to understand.

I strapped my camera around my neck and walked on. Not everything was meant to be photographed.

I had parked right by a streetlight and once my car was in sight I noticed how it gleamed strangely, like it was under interrogation. I stopped in the middle of the empty street, raised my camera to my face.

On the way back to my apartment, I hit all the green lights, though I found myself wishing for a red because I had an uneasy feeling that something was in the backseat, cloaked in the shadows behind me.

At the complex, I parked and twisted around to check. Of course there was nothing.

It was three in the morning by the time I got home and in the stairwell I could still hear my neighbor wailing. I went to her door and knocked so hard my knuckles stung. The door swung open and there she stood, the wailing woman, her chest heaving, her face luminous and swollen, in denim shorts and a giant black T-shirt. She looked at once relieved and appalled to see me.

"What is wrong?" I said to her. "What is so very wrong?"

She squinted at me like I was dense, her eyes bloodshot and leaking. "What isn't wrong?"

I watched the news. I couldn't argue.

"How much longer do you plan to keep this up? All night you go on. I can't sleep."

"You should try sleeping during the day."

"I have a job," I said. "Do you not have a job?"

"Not all jobs are done during the day."

I couldn't understand what kind of job my neighbor could be doing in her apartment in the middle of the night, with all that wailing.

"I was just about to take a break." She snapped the purple hair elastic on her wrist. "Do you want to come in?"

I *did* want to go in, to my surprise; it had been a long while since I had spent time in another person's home, so lonely that maybe I had started making up presences in the backseat.

Her apartment was neat and spare. A small burnt-orange sofa and a coffee table in the center of the living room, a standing lamp in a corner. A glass bowl filled with red apples sat on the fake marble kitchen island. On the coffee table, I noticed a head-set plugged into a cell phone, a thin black mike extending from the base. The headset was surrounded by boxes of tissues and eye drops and cherry throat lozenges.

I sat on the edge of the couch. My neighbor brought over two clay mugs of tea. As she passed one to me I tried to read her tattoo.

"All that we see or seem is but a dream within a dream," she said when she caught me looking. "Edgar Allan Poe, artist and degenerate."

I bowed my head over the tea, felt steam on my face. I repeated the phrase to myself, thinking about how when he died stretched out in the grass I had thought my life was over, but that didn't turn out to be right at all; rather the life I'd had was consumed by a life I never could have imagined living.

"So that's my job." She gestured at the headset with her mug. "The crying." She explained that ever since she was a child she had been able to cry on demand and in recent months she had parlayed this gift into an actual job. She took calls for a fetish hotline that catered to people who were sexually aroused by the sound of another person weeping.

"Dacryphilia," she said. "That's the technical name."

The wailing I had heard from my apartment sounded like something out of a Greek tragedy; I had a hard time believing it was all a performance, in the service of a paycheck.

"Why on earth," I said.

"Most people get off on trying to comfort me. *Take it easy now. One day at a time.* They say things like that. Every now and then I talk to someone who likes the suffering, who wants me to beg for stuff."

"Like what?"

She blew on her tea. "Like my life."

Without my neighbor's wailing the building seemed unusually quiet, even for the hour. I wondered if some people had moved out over the summer.

"So what do you do when you can't sleep?" my neighbor asked.

"I drive around and take pictures."

"Can I see?"

She pointed at my chest. I looked down and was startled to discover my camera; I had forgotten I was still wearing it around my neck.

I put my mug down on the coffee table and unhooked the camera strap. My neighbor sat next to me on the couch; she smelled of fruity body lotion and the faintest trace of cigarettes, even though I had not noticed a pack or an ashtray or any other paraphernalia in the apartment. I clicked through the photos, showing her the nighttime malls and highways, the sinkhole and the mother keeling before her son. I lingered on the teenagers fucking behind the foreclosed Victorian. In one photo the boy's naked back was a silver arch cutting up through the dark.

"Jesus," she said. "These are creepy."

After I clicked past the last photo, of my car gleaming like a little spaceship under the streetlight, my neighbor pressed her fingers to my wrist.

"Wait," she said. "What was that?"

"That's just my car." I went back to the photo.

"No." She tapped her fingernail against the small screen. "Right there. In the window."

The moment I hunched over the camera he appeared in the passenger window, trapped like a specimen in the glass. His face had a greenish tint, the borders bright and jellied, a liquid gone temporarily solid.

"A reflection," I could hear my neighbor saying. "Is that it?"

I did not know how to answer her. My breath was a thunder between my ears.

He was the same age as he was when I saw him last, that liminal meadow between boy and whatever was supposed to come next.

I clicked back through the Slumberland photos and then returned to my car and this time he looked a little different, his face distorted from being pressed too hard against the window, as though pained by having to wait for me to come back.

I decided the world was playing a terrible trick on me and the only solution would be to destroy my camera at once and maybe even my car too. Possibly I should never leave my apartment again and get a job that kept me indoors, like my neighbor.

First, though, I would have to get up.

"Could I lie down for a minute?" I asked my neighbor.

"Sure." She checked her watch. She stood and collected our mugs. "My break is up in five minutes, just so you know."

I stretched out on the soft beige carpet and held my camera against my stomach.

"This never happened," I said to her. "I never came here and showed you these photos."

"But you did." She stood over me, holding the mugs.

My neighbor disappeared into the kitchen. I heard the slap-slap of her bare feet. I heard the faucet turn on. When she returned, shaking water from her hands, she collected her headset and cell phone. She kneeled beside me and placed the phone just above my heart.

"Give it a try," she said. "People like it best when they know the pain is real."

She pressed the plastic band onto my skull and secured the headphones over my ears, positioned the mike so that I could feel the smooth edge brushing against my lip. She picked up my camera and strapped it around her own neck. She told me to get ready.

"What the fuck," I said to my neighbor, "is happening," but it was too late: there was already a voice on the line, breathing hard into the phone, saying *What are you waiting for, do it, come on.* The voice sounded muffled and strange, like it was being altered by a machine.

"Hello," I said to the voice. "I'm here."

Oh, if only this stranger could have heard me right after he died with grass under his head. I had gone on and on like my neighbor; my tears would have been the stuff of this caller's wildest, wettest dreams.

I tried to remember the feel of his hand in mine, always a bit sticky and warm in the way of little boys.

You weren't supposed to stay stuck with me, I thought. *You were supposed to be nothing or you were supposed to be free.*

Still, no tears. I remained a foot soldier in the long dry march of the after.

I asked the caller, "What do you think happens to us after we die?"

My neighbor sprawled out on her side, raised my camera to her face. "For posterity," she said, and then the shutter clicked.

One night, months in the future, I wouldn't hear a peep coming from my neighbor's apartment and the next morning I would knock on her door and discover that another person, a graduate student, had moved in. That was how things went in these big apartment complexes; they were a kind of purgatory where we docked until our souls were called elsewhere. I stopped taking photos around Slumberland after the body of a teenage girl was found inside the foreclosed Victorian, a nasty surprise for the rich couple who had bought the place. Because I never saw or shot her face I could not know if it was the same girl I'd photographed fucking in the grass, but I turned my camera over to the police anyway, desperate to be of use. "These are not illegal per se," an officer told me after reviewing the photos. "But they are troubling all the same."

In my neighbor's apartment, the phone was a hot weight on my chest and the caller was still panting.

"He was supposed to be nothing or he was supposed to be free," I said to the caller.

"Okay," said my neighbor. "That's enough of that." Her index finger hovered over the phone, preparing to put an end to her little experiment, my camera swinging from her neck.

"Why?" the caller roared just before the line went dead. Their voice came at me like a knife, sharp with rage and want. "Why do you not hurt?"

HILL OF HELL

had traveled up the Hudson at my friend's invitation, to deliver a lecture to his literature students at the college where he taught. There had been three people in attendance and one had fallen asleep halfway through. My friend had treated me to lunch before the lecture and to a drink afterward, so that by the time we hit the train back into the city we had sailed through the small talk and were ready for the blood and guts.

After we opened the second bottle of wine, which my friend had been carrying in his briefcase, I told him about the worst thing that had happened to me in the last three years, as this was the period of time that had elapsed since we last saw each other. We sat at a table in the café car, the panoramic windows looking out on the vast sweep of the Hudson. At first, I was surprised that we could drink our own alcohol openly on the train, but my friend assured me that we could eat and drink whatever we wanted because there was no food service on this route and besides he had been taking this train three days a week for a decade and knew every conductor on here and could get away with anything.

"It was around this time last year when everything came apart," I said, turning my plastic cup on the table.

For the lecture, I had traveled to New York from Boston, with the intent of spending several days visiting friends and museums, and the time alone had encouraged this memory to mushroom in my imagination, crowding everything else out.

Last September, I told my friend, I was pregnant. My husband had been the one wracked with longing for a child and I had allowed myself to be carried along by the tide of his enthusiasm, but once it was underway I felt like I had been conned into a heist for which, as the plans came into focus, I was woefully unprepared. You're talking about robbing the Louvre and I'm just a common criminal! In those early weeks, I willed my body to show up with the getaway car and then six months later, after I had forgotten all about getaway cars, I was standing in an Ikea in Stoughton, of all the undignified places, waving a spatula and lecturing my husband about how our dairy products were teeming with opiates, when my shorts filled with blood and I fainted. While I was unconscious, I had a dream that men in white coats were elbow deep in me and then I awoke in a hospital bed to find a doctor elbow deep in me, working on my body with the patient, grave air of an executioner. The baby had ten fingers and ten toes, the only thing that many a stranger had told me I should care about. Eyelids as thin as organza.

"She was stillborn," I said.

Now my husband wanted to try again, even after seeing his wife faint in a pool of blood and a dead child pulled from her body.

"Our marriage is on borrowed time," I told my friend.

The air-conditioning was out in our car. My friend mopped his forehead with a paper napkin. His hair sat like a white bush on his head and, despite the bifocals, his expression had tapered into a kind of eternal squint. He told me that in the last year his father, mother, and sister had all died. In six months' time, he had lost his entire family. He went on to say that his sister, the only person his mother had ever loved, died first and then his mother, the only person his father had ever loved, died second and then it was just my friend and his father and they had never liked each other very much at all.

"The big alone," he said. "That's all any of us has in the end. Nothing can protect us from it, not careers or children or spouses or money or lovers."

When I asked my friend if he was telling me that nothing matters, if at this stage he had embraced outright nihilism, he replied, "What I'm saying is: you can't change the essential outcome." Then he went quiet and I could tell he was watching something over my shoulder. He flung his arms across the table and leaned in close. "The conductor is coming. I'm warning you." We had our tickets, so I couldn't see a reason to be frightened of the conductor, and I wondered if my friend had already gotten a bit too drunk.

As if on cue, the conductor appeared at the head of our little table. He was a young man, with pink cheeks and a buzz cut, and his face did not yet betray the deadening repetition of having traveled the same stretch of river a million times over. Even the Hudson could lose its beauty if you were forced to look upon it for too long.

"Here's the latest." The conductor brandished his phone. "He's gained five pounds."

I peered down at the screen, only to behold the ugliest baby I had ever seen, hairless and shriveled as a raisin, his tiny mouth contorted as though in response to the myriad horrors of this world.

"Wow," I said, thinking that my friend had been right to warn me. "That's really something."

The conductor beamed and then continued down the aisle, pausing to scan tickets. Whenever the small talk with a passenger went on for a bit, he would take out his phone and beam some more.

"The poor bastard," my friend said. "He has no idea."

The outside world disappeared, replicated by a shadow network of track and tunnel. Passengers began to fold newspapers, gather bags, rise from seats. My friend slipped on the sports coat he'd worn to class, despite the heat.

"The big alone," he said, shaking a finger like the old professor he was becoming. "Don't ever forget about it."

I had expected for us to have a proper goodbye in the station, given how long it had been since we'd seen each other and the intensity of our respective losses, which we had shared so freely. I had expected us to embrace, for him to thank me for coming and me to thank him for having me, no matter how small the stipend or the audience. The real remuneration had been the time spent together, the chance to get caught up. You reach a certain point in life and you go too long without seeing someone you care for and the next thing you know they're dead. But I had forgotten that we were arriving at rush hour and as we pressed our way out of the train we were separated. I could glimpse the silvered peak of my friend's head, his jacket collar upturned like a fin. *Wait*, I thought. *Surely there is something else.* On the platform, I saw him look back once, right as he stepped onto the escalator. He gave me a little wave and for a moment I thought he was going to fight his way back down, but then the woman behind my friend flapped her arms, implored him to get moving, and so he chose to push on.

■   ■   ■

Six months after my friend and I rode the train together, I left my husband. Some years later, I remarried. My friend was invited to the wedding, held in an arboretum in Jamaica Plain, but he was too ill to attend. He sent me a note of congratulations and that was the last time I heard from him before he died. In my second marriage, I was the one who lobbied for a child and when I gave birth to a daughter, I thought the universe had granted me a chance to remake my life. The notion of being at the mercy of the universe turned me superstitious in a way I had never been before—for example, for the duration of my pregnancy and my daughter's childhood I never once set foot inside an Ikea and was better for it.

It pains me to say that our daughter was, from the moment of her birth, a difficult human being. A sleepless and squalling baby, possessed by violent tantrums as an older child, episodes where she hit and kicked and bit. Twice I needed stitches. In high school, she was diagnosed with a mood disorder. She wanted to write but could never get organized enough to make anything. She dropped out of college and got mixed up with drugs and when we finally staggered out of that terrible wilderness, marked by disappearances and theft and countless lies, the sober version of my daughter turned out to be just as prone to petty cruelty and deception. I wondered if something was genetically wrong with me, given that my body had killed one daughter in the womb and produced another so maladapted. I confess that when my daughter first complained of fatigue and back pain keeping her from work I thought she might be up to her old tricks, that she was waking too hungover to get to her job answering phones at a veterinary clinic, but then an MRI revealed a malignant tumor burrowed deep in her spine like a fat white tick and we were lost to the equally terrible wilderness of chemotherapy and radiation and drug trials, of oceanic despair and hope as fragile as eggshell. Just after my daughter's thirty-third birthday her oncologist sat us all down in his office with the latest test results and said there was nothing left to do except prepare.

At the height of our daughter's troubles, after a hair-raising visit to her third rehab facility, my husband, once we were back in the car, had pounded the steering wheel and wept and cried out, *I never wanted this. Why can't she just leave us be?* After that meeting with the oncologist, I wondered in secret if my husband felt the soul-warping shame that I had years ago, when my body became the getaway car I had begged it to be after all. I have learned that one must be very careful about the desperate wishes cast out into the ether because perhaps someone is listening, someone all too willing to grant us exactly what we have asked for and maybe even what we deserve.

When my daughter began palliative care, I thought nonstop about what my friend had told me on the train, about the big alone, but the strange thing was that I had never seen her so awash in company. She had embraced the "positive death" movement, introduced to her when she took a six-week course called the Art of Dying. She was a regular at death cafés and at the meeting my daughter asked me to attend, so I could better understand her philosophy of dying, I was able to discern that some of the participants were sick and not getting better and some were from medical or religious communities and some were morbidly curious or worse. One man asked questions that made me

strongly suspect he had necrophilic leanings; a woman who vol-
unteered to sit with the dying in hospice announced, with her
eyes closed and her hands in a steeple, that the end of life experience was "more transcendent than an orgasm." I could not get
away from these people fast enough. My daughter decided on a
green burial, which meant that her body, unembalmed, would
be interned in a biodegradable casket and we would plant a lin-
den tree in place of a headstone. She hired an end-of-life doula,
who claimed that birth and death were more or less the same:
seminal life experiences that most approached with witless terror. Our daughter rented out a bar and threw her own celebra-
tion of life party. Among the guests we recognized few people
from her world as it had existed before dying the best death
possible became her full-time job. Instead the place was flooded
with these death enthusiasts, who kept coming up to us, her
bewildered parents, and saying deeply surprising things about
our daughter: the beautiful song she had written for someone's
funeral; the prayer circles she led; the homemade soups and
juices she brought to people who were dying or grieving or just
plain sick and tired of being here.

Where had this individual been when she was well? I thought
as I watched these people embrace our daughter, who looked
serene and beautiful in a floor-length white peasant dress. She
was barefoot. She wore a crown of daises on her head, like a
forest nymph. Was this the person she had been all along, and
we had somehow failed to coax this kinder self out into the
world?

Of course, I knew my thoughts about my daughter's new
community were ungenerous, but this was how I had come to
understand the big alone—the way we are walled in by our secrets and the implacability of our judgments. The big alone had

little to do with physical company; rather it was a matter of understanding, and where understanding broke down.

"We should abide whatever brings her comfort," my husband always insisted. He was so shattered by the whole situation that he had lost the ability to think critically. Meanwhile, I could not help but feel betrayed by the universe; as it turned out, I had been doomed to relive the same old story, with the same ending, even if that ending arrived at a different moment in time. I'd never told my husband about my stillborn daughter, so I had no one with whom I could discuss this brutal symmetry. I no longer knew how to contact my first husband, who last I heard had moved to Europe for work, and my friend was, by then, long dead.

In our daughter's last week on earth, we slept in cots in her hospital room. The day of the week, the hour of the day—time in the conventional sense had become meaningless; the only clock I could track was how many breaths she had taken and how many more she had left. There were long stretches of silence, all of us engaged in our private acts of bargaining. I had spent my life studying medieval literature and I thought often of the Basilica of Saint Francis of Assisi, how before the construction began, just after Saint Francis's canonization in 1228, the site had been used for public executions and was known as the Hill of Hell. Because the laborers believed the hilltop to be contagious with doom, they refused to work on the basilica and so the pope offered anyone who would forty days off their stay in purgatory and that was how the Basilica of Saint Francis of Assisi came to be built. I thought about how few things were more ancient than the bartering of souls.

One night, out of nowhere, I remembered the train conductor on the Hudson. In my imagination, he was still a young man and his baby was still a baby and ugly as can be. But of course the conductor would be much older now and his child would be an adult and perhaps it was like in a fairy tale and his son had grown into the most handsome man in all of New York.

I left my daughter's room and decided I would go over to maternity and see if I could look at some babies, but after wandering a series of hallways and getting turned around by signs I realized that the babies were kept in a separate building, one that I couldn't reach at this hour. The next time I saw the death doula I was going to pull her aside and demand to know why, if birth and death were so very similar, they were not permitted to occur in the same space.

In my daughter's room, I found her twitching under the thin hospital blanket. Her eyelids were fluttering. Her open mouth had the look of a small, dark cave. My husband was still asleep on his cot, curled and facing a blank wall. I wondered if it might be time for more morphine soon and if so, how long it would take a nurse to get around to administering it. I placed a finger under her left eye and felt her lashes brush my skin. When I was certain she could not hear me, I kneeled beside her bed and said, "You were not my first child. You had a sister, a long time ago, but she did not make it very far in this life." I don't know why I so badly needed to tell my daughter the truth, right there at the end. Maybe I thought she deserved to know that her mother was not always what she appeared to be—and that maybe I, as her mother, deserved someone to tell.

When I turned from her bedside, I saw that my husband was not asleep at all. He was sitting on the edge of his cot, facing me, his shoulders square, his hands clamped on his knees. He was starting to look a little like my friend had on the train, all those years ago: the squint, the shock of white. I sat down next to him, expecting to have to answer for what he had just overhead, which would frankly have been a relief, a chance to talk about these twin losses and how our most cloistered wishes and our ultimate fates might or might not be related. Is any thought truly private or is everything overheard by a presence we cannot detect? If nature loves symmetry then why is symmetry so cruel? But my husband never said a word about it—not then and not later. I think it must have been too much for him to take in. Instead we slept the rest of the night in the same cot, our arms wrapped tight and hot around each other, and even today I could not guess at his thoughts.

CULT OF MARY

As we entered Arezzo, the guide pointed out the prostitutes lining the road. The women looked like awkward, flashy birds, teetering in bright spandex and spike heels, flimsy gold jewelry flashing in the summer sun. A man in our group made a joke about wanting to stop and check their prices—to see how they stacked up against the pleasure of a fine gelato—and the guide, still speaking into her little microphone, said that these women were impoverished and in some cases stateless, that their trade was born of survival and they deserved our respect.

At that, the man sank back into his seat, let out a little huff.

The trip had been organized by the local chapter of my mother's university club and this man wasted no time making enemies. In Rome, there were the lewd comments about the statues of naked women. At lunch, he drank too much and broke into song, off-key American power ballads. He claimed to be fluent in Italian, but we had yet to hear him speak a word. At every available opportunity he reminded us that he'd planned to take this trip with his wife, who was now three months dead, ensuring we all felt held hostage by obligatory sympathy.

In Arezzo, we parked and followed the guide up a steep stone street, curving in the direction of Piazza Grande, and that was when we realized this man, our common enemy, had peeled away from the group. Perhaps he had gone to check the prices after all.

"Maybe he'll like Arezzo so much he won't want to leave," my mother said, locking onto my arm with her wizened hands, the skin craggy and spotted in a way that made me think of clay.

"We'll never get that lucky," I said back.

The guide was a young woman with a lip ring and a curly-haired mohawk. She had the unflappable calm of a seasoned camp counselor and did not seem overly concerned that one of her charges had wandered away.

"Half the time the prostitutes just take the men into the woods and rob them," our guide remarked. "Or sometimes they perform witchcraft and cast spells. If that's where he went, he'll come back with a strange and memorable story."

This guide was full of strange and memorable stories herself. On the drive over from Florence, she had revealed to us the Tuscan secret to flower gardens: wrap a strand of your own hair around the root tendrils and plant on the night of a waxing—never a waning—moon, prompting my mother to comment that she kept a flourishing rose garden for years and never once had to get her own hair involved.

My mother had been looking forward to Italy ever since her club announced the trip. She cut her spending in preparation, downgrading her cable package and declining invitations to go out to eat. For Christmas, I bought her a new suitcase, a sleek hard-shell roller, though when the time came she had insisted on using her ancient cloth suitcase with a broken wheel because it held more. *It doesn't hold more*, I'd tried to tell her, *it only seems like it holds more*; at that, my mother had looked up from folding shirts and regarded me as though I had been seized by madness.

On New Year's Eve, I went to a party with a tarot reader, a man who examined my cards and told me, his face pinched with sorrow, that my mother would be dead within the year—and then in the damp chill of early spring she had a stroke, and though she would recover in time for the trip, we both agreed she should not travel on her own, so here I was in the Duomo di Arezzo, waiting for my mother to lean over and whisper that she couldn't understand the guide, the girl's accent was too thick and she was speaking too quickly, and why did she have to wear her hair like that anyway. My mother had never understood women who chose against conventional prettiness. Every day I had woken with a leaden sadness because I knew in my heart that this was the last trip my mother would ever take and Italy was all she had wanted (for months a Tuscan field had been the background on her phone) and now that she was here, nothing pleased her. If it wasn't the guide, it was the heat or the uneven streets or no washcloths in the hotel or no ice in the restaurants or the boorish man who had recently lost his wife and had possibly abandoned our group for the company of stateless and impoverished roadside prostitutes. And of course we had set ourselves up for this failure, the two of us, for how could any trip, no matter how splendid, bear up under the brutal weight of *last*?

As we moved down an aisle in a hush, the guide pointed out a statue of Christ that had been carved from a single block of wood. By a Piero della Francesca fresco of Mary Magdalene, the guide explained that long ago the church became anxious about the Cult of Mary and their secretive powers, so they had allowed the legacies of all the different Marys to be conflated, which meant now most people didn't know the difference between Mary of Clopas and Mary of Bethany and Mary of Jacob; apparently this confusion had been the church's intention all along. I wondered if the vaulted position Mary Magdalene held in the Duomo explained why so many prostitutes flocked to Arezzo.

"Remember that history is not only about what happened," the guide added, "but also about what those in power want you to think happened."

Back in Piazza Grande, I overheard a white couple muttering that they wished the guide would lay off the feminist politics.

In the van, we had been given itineraries and I thought that maybe the missing man would turn up outside the Duomo, sweaty and smug, but I did not see him anywhere as we made our way down the twisting streets, past a park with five bronze sheep grazing on grass banks.

The guide waved her small red flag, alerting us to our next stop.

"These are fascist sheep," she told us.

"How can sheep be fascist?" someone objected. "Sheep don't believe in anything."

The guide explained that Mussolini had initiated a tax credit for anyone in Tuscany who owned sheep, not because they were practically useful but rather because sheep-dotted fields and hillsides fit Mussolini's pastoral ideal of the Italian countryside. The bronze sheep had been erected in Arezzo to commemorate this policy.

"That is how evil first creeps in," she went on. "Through the falsification of beauty."

She told us that evil rarely looked like evil when it first arrived. It could look like innovation and progress and prosperity, courage even, but more than anything it looked, to some, like a solution—a solution to the secret problem they believed had gone too long unaddressed. They felt as though they had been speaking a hidden language among themselves, and then a man or a woman in a suit stood on a stage and addressed cheering masses in that very same language, hidden no longer.

The guide paused, breathless, and jabbed her red flag at the sheep.

We pressed on. Behind me the couple who had objected to the guide's feminist politics were now plotting word for word the terrible review they planned to leave her on TripAdvisor. *Why is some person, everywhere you go, always demanding that you pick a side?* At the bottom of a hill, we found the missing man sitting at a bus stop, a good distance away from where the prostitutes congregated. His clothes were rumpled and smeared with dirt; leaves stuck out of his hair like ornaments on a tree. He was missing his shoes. As a group, we approached him, demanded to know where he had been and what had happened. The man told us that he had followed two women into the woods, to a mattress under a tree, but before they did anything they wanted half their money, which he handed right over, and then they wanted to know how many Marys he could name.

"I said the Mary who gave birth to Jesus and then that other Mary who was a prostitute, but give me a break, I was raised by atheists and I couldn't think of any more damn Marys. They started pelting me with handfuls of dirt and sticks. They knocked me down and stole my shoes and drove me out of the woods."

The guide began to laugh and applaud, her face slashed by a wild grin. "Of all the tours for you to miss!" she exclaimed.

"My wife's not really dead," the man said next, in flawless Italian, which shocked everyone. "She just left me and sometimes I feel like I've forgotten how to breathe."

He sank his face into his palms and began to sob, his shoulders heaving. The guide helped him up and led him over to a water fountain, the kind that looks like a beautiful little iron hydrant with a spout, so he could wash his feet, his soles caked with mud and leaves. The guide rejoined the group on the opposite side of the street and together we watched this man struggle. First he tried standing on one leg and holding a foot into the stream, but then he started to wobble, so next he squatted and bent his leg into the water, like he was attempting a yoga pose. My mother leaned against me; I knew that soon she would be looking for a place to sit down. "Where's Mary Magdalene when you need her?" someone said, but they were shushed by the rest of the group. We all knew we were witnessing a holy scene. Finally the man just stood in front of the fountain and let the water coat his feet, his back to us, shoulders still trembling.

On the ride to San Marino, the van was warm and quiet and soon my mother slumped over into sleep. We both knew that she was too frail to be touring Italy and our shared knowledge of her weakness made her enraged by her own body, which in turn made her enraged by all the places that had no interest in accommodating bodies such as hers. I wished the club had announced this trip many years in the past. Near Sansepolcro, I watched my mother's hand twitch in her lap and I hoped that she was not yet dreaming of death, but of gardeners wrapping strands of their own hair around dirt-clotted roots and fascist sheep and a life carved from a single block of wood and a man struggling to wash the shame from his feet.

LIZARDS

The judge is still in the news. The story has been unfolding for weeks and every time she sees his face she feels so angry she's surprised surfaces don't ignite when she touches them. By dinnertime, a third woman has come forward. She and her husband eat in front of the blaring TV, plates balanced on their laps, forks suspended in midair. Afterward they do the dishes, standing barefoot in their small kitchen, the news still droning in the background. He washes and she dries because she keeps cracking wineglasses; in the last week they have gone from six to two. The kitchen is a shotgun, with a yellow tile floor and an outdated light fixture and a refrigerator that shudders and whines. They keep meaning to call someone to come out and have a look at the fridge, but then life intervenes and no calls get made.

"He should be in prison," she says, toweling a plate. One thing about living in an apartment complex is that you're always listening to a network of lives unfold around you and right now she can hear water running upstairs. She imagines a different couple washing dishes together, what they might be discussing. Lizards, perhaps. How they don't have eyelids and can shed their tails at will and how they smell by tasting the air around them.

They have lived in Florida for only six months, but already she hates lizards, almost as much as she hates her new job. Entry-level, securities corporation, hellish commute. She dreams of having more money, more time, more space.

"Probably so." Her husband pauses. He is concerned about the fridge too—the humming is louder than usual and he would be at wit's end if the appliance broke down altogether; there is far too much he needs to keep cool. Also, a sharp and unfamiliar pain keeps flaring in his left heel, probably from all the waiting. They moved south for his job, his big opportunity, and then he was laid off before they could even finish furnishing the apartment and he didn't expect to still be looking, but he is. In the meantime, he made a profile on a task app and discovered a great demand for taskers who could wait. Say you wanted barbecue from the popular place that did not deliver or concert tickets or the latest Apple product and you did not want to wait in line— well, why bother when you could hire someone like him to do the waiting for you.

"That's all you have to say?" She can tell he's holding back, from the way he keeps shifting his weight around, eyes flitting from sink to fridge, anywhere but her face.

He weighs his options, decides to press on. "Well—"

"Well *what*?"

"It's just that nothing has been proven yet."

They both left dirty dishes in the sink that morning, so they have a whole mess of washing ahead. Sometimes she wakes so bleary she can't do anything more than stagger into the shower and dress, her blouse buttoned crooked half the time. She has stopped blow-drying her hair or putting on makeup, save for a slash of lipstick applied in the rearview on her way to work. They don't even have kids yet and she is already so tired, which worries her, though her husband blames the era that they live in—so divisive, so exhausting, who could keep up—and says they should spend less time watching the news.

"Okay." She adds the plate to the dry rack. All week she has been preparing for this very conversation. "Let's say two of the women are lying. Let's just say. That still leaves one who is telling the truth. One is enough. Right?"

"Of course." He raises the dripping sponge. He has learned to proceed carefully during these kinds of conversations. Ever since the allegations were made against the judge, the hostile nature of the news has started to leak into his wife; she's like a boxer these days, always out there with that jab. He tries to channel the calm he feels while waiting in line. He is a good waiter, patient and focused, though in general the taskers are less agitated than the people doing their own waiting. For the taskers there is nothing on the other side of the waiting; the waiting is what they are there to do.

"I'm just saying we can't become so emotional, so caught up in the moment, that we forget about evidence. Corroboration and so on. I'm not saying he's innocent. I'm just saying he hasn't been *proven* guilty. Not yet, anyway."

She picks up a fork. He goes to work scrubbing a pot. The pain in his heel travels up the back of his leg like an electrical current; he tries to remember when exactly the discomfort first started. Was it last week, when he waited in line for three hours to collect tickets for a country music concert?

"Have you ever—"

She stops short, feels the fork tines through the dish towel. She has practiced asking him this question in their bathroom mirror and in the rearview and in the compact she keeps in her purse.

"Have I ever what?"

"Have you ever been at a party where things got out of hand?"

"Well, I *was* in a fraternity." He smiles at the memories of drinking shirtless and barefoot in the backyard of a house that no one person owned but everyone seemed to live in.

"Okay, so at one of those parties, did you ever—"

"Did I ever *what*?"

"Did you ever hear about stuff happening? Like with other guys in the fraternity?"

They're edging into tricky territory, if he's being honest. Sure, there were whisperings, here and there. The parties could get rowdy. A girl could maybe get touched in a way she wasn't expecting (a sudden and unwelcome memory: his hand grazing a first year's ass, which had looked so delicious in her jeans, and the girl whipping around, indignant, and him slurring, *Where do you think you are?*)

"Look," he says, loud enough to be heard over the ambient noise of neighbors and the humming fridge. "I'm not saying everyone was an angel back then. That we wouldn't do some things a little differently now. All I'm saying is that there's a difference between having a regret or two and committing an actual *crime*."

"I guess it depends on what's being regretted," she replies.

"It's just that, in this day and age, a simple mistake or a misunderstanding, made years in the past, when you were a completely different person, can be called up at any time to ruin someone's life. Does that seem reasonable to you?"

"He's going to be on the Supreme Court," she says. "His life is hardly ruined."

They work in thick, humid silence for a while. He passes her a glass salad bowl, a wedding gift. The bowl is big and slips around in her arms.

"What about you?" she says.

"What about me?"

"Have you ever—"

The next question she has not practiced aloud. It bursts from her, a detonation. She hugs the bowl and stares down through the bottom, the tile floor warped by the glass.

This time, the jab connects. The fridge hums louder; he implores himself to not rush over to the white door and investigate further. He feels genuinely wounded by the question and also like if he does not respond in just the right way, with the right amounts of shock and sadness and indignation, he will, despite being entirely innocent, be implicated in his wife's eyes.

He flings the sponge in the sink and turns off the water. He tries to keep both his feet planted on the floor, even as his heel throbs. "How could you even ask me that?"

The glass bowl is too big for the dry rack, so she places it on top of the microwave. She slings the dish towel over her shoulders and crosses her arms.

"Well," she says. "Why didn't you?"

"Because I was raised right! Because I'm a decent person! Because I have a *sister*, for Christ's sake." He imagines his heel burning a hole in the floor, a small and perfect circle, lined with ash. He waits for her to say something more, to apologize, and when she doesn't he adds, "We have really got to stop watching the news. It's making you paranoid."

"Turn the water back on," she says. "I'd like to be done before midnight."

"Be careful." He hands her a wineglass.

As she dries the glass, her eyes wander over to the empty

wall, where they keep meaning to hang a watercolor of daises in a jar that they bought at a yard sale. She is staring at that blank space when a green garden lizard darts across. It pauses for a moment, cocks its tiny head, and then shoots behind the kitchen cabinet. She shrieks and drops the wineglass.

"Shit!" he cries out, louder than he means to. "I *told* you to be careful." At this rate, they'll be drinking wine from coffee mugs by the weekend.

"Didn't you see that lizard?" She crouches down and picks up a long glass shard, her heart still quaking. "It ran right across the wall."

"No. I did not." He fetches the broom and sweeps up the glass. He tells her to step aside; if she tries to touch the glass she'll only cut herself. Does he have to do everything around here? "But do you know what? I see lizards every day. And do you know why? Because lizards are everywhere around here. They are everywhere and they are perfectly harmless."

She knows the lizards are harmless—they aren't poisonous, they don't have teeth—but she is from up north and she can't get used to these creatures crawling around inside her apartment. They look like tiny dinosaurs and tiny dinosaurs do not belong in people's homes. Their apartment is on the sixth floor—how do they even get up here?

"I need to go for a walk," she says.

Her husband will not approve—no one they know in Florida treats walking as a leisure activity—but she is desperate for air. They live in one of those labyrinthine apartment complexes ringed by interstates, but she can at least wander the grounds and the parking lots and sit out by the retention pond. Sometimes, in the stairwells, she even finds interesting things to observe. Once she glimpsed a spectacular moth—orange and gold, a black dot on each wing—batting against a light. Also, if she's out past a certain hour, she hears the same neighbor weeping in her apartment. It sounds like the neighbor is having a nervous breakdown in there, night after night. Sometimes she lingers by the door and listens for a minute, just to keep her own life in perspective. It has never occurred to her to knock.

"Wait." He hates this walking habit she insists on clinging to. Once, not long after they moved and he learned that she'd gone on foot to the grocery, he had to take her aside and let her know that around here only poor people walked—a crass thing to say, perhaps, but it was the truth.

"I won't be long." She picks up the remote and turns off the TV.

"Have you been hydrating?" He opens the fridge and reaches for a can of sparkling water, lime-flavored. He holds it out to his wife. She stares at the can for a moment and when she finally accepts it she doesn't open the water right away—she just holds the can to her forehead and shuts her eyes. It's only when she turns and enters the living room that he hears the reassuring hiss of the tab popping.

He heard about this sparkling water from another husband in the complex, who maintains a stockpile in the trunk of his car. One Saturday afternoon, they were drinking beers by the retention pond and started complaining about their wives. *It is a universal truth*, the neighbor said, *that some women never know when to shut the fuck up*. He laughed along, even though his neighbor's brashness made him uncomfortable. He likes to think of himself as more evolved. He's a registered Democrat. He wore a DEAL ME IN T-shirt to the polls on Election Day. *Come on*, the neighbor said next. *I want to show you something.* In the parking lot, the neighbor popped open his trunk, cut into a flat of cans, and passed him one. It was lukewarm and looked like off-brand LaCroix. *Have her drink it,* he said, *and then call me in the morning.* The neighbor assured him that his wife drank a can almost every night and she was as healthy as a horse—healthier, even, than she'd been before. Besides, this water would be everywhere before too long, according to the neighbor; they needed new defenses for these times. So he took a can to be neighborly and planned to dispose of the water but then his wife came in from work, looking pale and disheveled, her blouse crooked, and started in about how she had been thinking and maybe Florida wasn't working out for them and she really did hate her job and all this driving was frying her nerves and maybe they needed to move back north because she just couldn't imagine starting a family here and—

"Is that LaCroix?" she said after he opened the fridge and handed her a cold can.

"Even better," he said back.

He went into the bathroom to shower and when he returned his wife was unconscious in bed, sunk into a deep and peaceful slumber, the half-empty can sitting on the bedside table. In the morning, she woke refreshed and cheerful. That evening, she did not complain about the traffic or her job.

On his lunch break, he called his neighbor and demanded to know where this magical sparkling water had come from. His neighbor said that he had heard about it from another husband in a different apartment complex who heard about it from a second cousin who heard about it from an Internet forum. *For a small fee,* his neighbor said, *I can be your supplier.*

That was two months ago.

Now each time his wife simply becomes *too much* he offers her a can of sparkling water. He tells her it's artisanal, made in small batches by a family friend who likes to gift it around. It helps that they live in Florida, where everyone is overheated all the time. He clips out articles on the importance of hydration for skin elasticity and weight loss and a general sense of well-being from women's magazines and drops them into her purse.

"I might not go for a walk after all," his wife calls out from the living room. "I just got *so* sleepy."

She stands slumped in front of the silent TV and spends five minutes debating whether or not to brush her teeth before eventually deciding she is so desperate for sleep she must go straight to bed, hygiene be damned.

Of course, she has noticed a correlation between drinking the sparkling water, with the mysterious label she can never find anywhere else, and being seized by a narcoleptic longing for sleep. She believes the story about the family friend, even if making small-batch artisanal water does seem like a curious way to spend one's time. But she likes the word *artisanal*, thinks it sounds aspirational, and also the water is just so refreshing. Lately, though, she's started to get an icy feeling in her stomach whenever her husband hands her a can and at the same time, for reasons she cannot articulate to herself, she feels compelled to accept his offering, as though they have entered into an agreement she doesn't quite understand. Also, there is the problem of how her sleep has changed. After drinking the water, she used to wake feeling as though she had slept for a hundred years, like a character in a fairy tale, but recently she has been coming to in the middle of the night, upright in the shower or in the kitchen, her head stuck in the arctic glow of the freezer—even though she has no history of sleepwalking (her husband, always a sound sleeper, has yet to notice). Still, she wants this life. She really does, even if she has to admit that ever since the judge entered into the news cycle something inside her has been disturbed. The women who have come forward—they are so *relatable*. One of them looks just like her aunt Karen. So she wants to stand up. She wants to do something. If only she weren't so tired. She should go to a march! Instead she has started shouting at the drivers who cut her off in traffic and snapping at coworkers and picking fights with her poor husband, who is trying his best, she supposes, to navigate these new currents.

The truth is that she is angriest at her own anger, which she suspects has arrived far too late to be of any real use.

She has been kept too safe, been too protected, for too long.

Besides, if she squints at the label the can just looks like a LaCroix.

This is what I need, she thinks as she sinks into bed. *This is what the world needs. Sleep is holy. Maybe our problems would be solved if everyone just got more sleep. Isn't that what the woman from the* Huffington Post *has been trying to tell us?* She drifts away listening to her husband bang around in the kitchen, his movements a dim echo through the wall.

The last time he bought a flat of cans from his neighbor, in a remote corner of one of the complex's many parking lots, the neighbor asked if he was taking "full advantage" of his new marital situation. He frowned and said he didn't know what that was supposed to mean and then the neighbor told him that when his wife drinks a full can you can't wake her up for the end of the world. *Call me twisted*, his neighbor whispered, *but it makes me feel like a ghost. Like I'm walking through walls while everyone else is still using doors.*

The neighbor's confession *was* twisted, he assures himself in the kitchen. Why would anyone want to be a ghost? In the parking lot, he yanked the flat from his neighbor's arms and hurried away, but now that the notion is in his head he can't scrub it out, especially when she kicks away the covers and he spots a smooth thigh all twisted up in the sheets.

Sometimes he wonders what would happen if everyone were to one day stop pretending and he feels afraid.

He searches for a way to roust out the lizard. He knows how to catch it in a water glass and release it back into the outdoors, if an apartment complex entombed by interstates could still be considered the outdoors. He's from this odd southern state and lizard catching was a favored pastime as a boy. He slams the cabinet doors open and shut, to see if he can startle the creature out from hiding. He pushes his fingers into the blade-narrow space between the cabinet and the wall. He looks forward to telling his wife that he stayed up very late and worked very hard to expel this lizard from their apartment, all in the service of her comfort.

She can't be sure of the time when she rises from bed and begins to move (quietly, quietly), out the front door and down the open stairwell and into a vast parking lot, the asphalt lunar under the fluorescents. She walks and she walks. She has the sensation of floating, which morphs into the sensation of having been halved, like a cell dividing. One version of herself is floating *right here* while another hovers in the distance, her pale blue nightgown fluttering at her ankles. Except she doesn't own a pale blue nightgown, she sleeps in sweats and T-shirts, and that's when she feels the burn of the asphalt on her bare feet and understands the woman in the distance is not a splinter of her self but rather a distinct person, out on her own night sojourn. She drifts closer to the woman; she imagines the two of them orbiting the parking lot together, twin satellites in outer space. She wants to call to the woman, to ask what she's doing out here, and then she feels the sound of her own voice ring through her like a bell. She stops walking. The distant woman pauses, turns toward her. She is so close to being awake.

He thinks he hears a door open and close; for a moment, he imagines a human-size lizard creeping into the apartment, but of course there are only two human-size creatures in here and he is in the kitchen and his wife is in bed, asleep.

He takes a break and searches for "agonizing heel pain" on his phone. The results include plantar fasciitis, cysts, tendon tears, nerve entrapment, gout. His phone buzzes in his hand, a notification from the app, to wait at the new Cronut place first thing tomorrow. He has a job interview lined up for next week, at a real estate company, and he hopes he gets hired. In his heart he knows waiting in line is an absurd and humiliating job for an adult to have and he tries to not think about what it means that he's so good at it.

When he finally catches the lizard, he doesn't slide his palm under the glass right away. He keeps the glass pressed to the wall and leers at his specimen. He knows he must look like a giant, from the lizard's perspective, that he must be terrifying. The creature is so still and it is strange how they watch you, with those unblinking eyes. Isn't it true that they don't have eyelids? Just as well, he thinks. They are little things, no longer than a finger, and so they have to be vigilant. The lizard cracks open its tiny mouth, heart twitching under its thin reptilian hide. His breath starts to fog the glass. It really does look like something from another epoch. *Prehistoric*, as his wife would say. *Why are there tiny dinosaurs in our home?* "How did you get all the way up here?" he asks the lizard, and the whole history of the world answers back.

THE PITCH

n the childhood photo my husband showed me, I noticed something strange. He had found the photo in a wood crate filled with his father's things. We had driven several such crates home with us after the funeral in Lake City, two weeks earlier. In the picture, my husband was standing in the woods, shirtless and barefoot and holding a fishing rod. Thirteen years old, slender and pale, a streak of mud on his cheek, one of his father's too-big belts knotted around his waist. Americana all the way.

My husband's mother, I had been told, died in childbirth. When we first met, he had a nasty habit of leaving his dirty socks on the bathroom floor and when I'd asked him, "Were you raised in the woods or what?" he had replied, "As a matter of fact I was."

The woods in the photo were called the Pitch, because the tree cover was so dense not even the fabled Florida sunshine could blunt the shadows. The first time my husband mentioned these woods—reachable on foot from his childhood home in North Florida—I'd asked him if the name had something to do with baseball and he'd said, "No, like pitch dark," and then I'd said, "As in Renata Adler?" and he'd looked at me like I was hopeless.

We went to the Pitch once and walked around in there, back when my husband's father was dying but not yet dead, and I'd wondered who was in charge of naming things, how such decisions were made.

I was fond of my father-in-law and had felt very sorry when he announced to us that he was dying, and remained sorry even after he began to flood my voicemail with messages, left in the middle of the night, in the last month of his life.

During this time, I had tried to engage my husband on the subject of his impending orphanhood, but he refused. Instead he spent his free hours cultivating his rose garden, examining the teas for signs of distress and pruning his floribundas; he ordered expensive mulches online and frequented a nearby slaughterhouse for fresh manure. From the window of my backyard studio I had observed him bending over the wide faces of the floribundas and whispering to them. Clearly he regarded the roses as superior confidants.

Yet I can't say that I was thinking about any of this when my husband showed me the photo. I was too busy looking at the boy in the background, small and white as milk and shimmying up a tree.

"Who's that?" I asked my husband, pressing my thumb over the boy's head. We were standing in my studio, just under a small skylight; all day I had been at work on an illustration project commissioned by a wealthy eccentric.

He snatched the photo from me. "What do you mean *who?* That's me. The man you married."

"Not *you*," I said, already exasperated. One unfortunate side effect of marriage was knowing the mistakes a person was going to make before they actually made them. I stood beside him and pointed at the boy in the tree.

He held the photo close to his face. He blinked like he had something in his eye. Had he really not noticed the boy until this very moment? It was summer, which meant everyone walked around looking like they'd just been sprayed with a hose, and yet when I touched my husband's arm his skin was cool and dry.

"I see what you're seeing." He began to nod. "I didn't before, but now I do."

He explained that the boy was not a boy at all, but rather a large vine wrapped around the tree trunk, bleached and distorted by exposure. He pushed the photo under my nose.

"Whatever you say." I returned to my desk, pressed a pencil to my sketchpad. I could feel my husband hovering over me, could hear him saying my name, but I did not look up—not if he was going to insist that I had mistaken a vine for a boy. That may have been the story he was intent on telling himself, but I wasn't about to let it infect me. I didn't yet understand that refusing one kind of narrative could activate another.

You draw one line and then you draw another, I told myself until I heard the studio door open and close, felt the air settle.

The next thing I knew it was dusk and I was standing by the window, at a momentary loss for how to proceed with the next phase of my illustration project, and my husband was in the backyard with a grill light and a shovel. I watched him set the photograph on fire and then bury the ashes in the ground, a safe distance from the roses.

■　■　■

After the incident with the photo, my husband's every movement adopted an aura of menace. I would look up from my desk and see his face pressed to the window of my studio or turn from the kitchen sink and find him right behind me in socked feet, perched on tiptoe like a gargoyle. He put his father's things on a shelf in the garage, too high for me to reach, especially now that our ladder seemed to have gone missing. My husband worked as a receptionist for a psychiatrist, Dr. X, and began coming home late. From bed, I would hear the car rumble into the driveway and once he was beside me I would, somewhat against my will, fall into a sleep so deep it was like being absorbed into a black hole, though I couldn't say that I ever felt "at rest." My husband continued to spend all his free time fussing over his roses. He started wearing his green gardening gloves indoors, leaving dirt trails on counters and side tables, charting his path through the house.

When he was around, he pestered me with strange questions. "Have you been checked for cataracts?" he asked one morning, peeling an orange with his gloved hands. "Have you ever suffered from psychodynamic visual hallucinations?" he asked another.

"Is that something you heard from Dr. X?" I said back. "Do you even know what those words mean?" My husband had always called his employer Dr. X and I had joined him in this practice because in a marriage few things were more powerful than shared habits. And then some years ago, at the office holiday party, I learned that everyone called him Dr. X—shorthand for a name, the doctor told me, he had grown tired of people mispronouncing.

"I don't understand what the big commotion is all about," I said to my husband in our kitchen. "I saw what I saw and I saw a boy in that tree."

My husband had never been the kind of person who demanded that everyone agree with his version of things, but perhaps he was turning into one. I told myself that he had been terribly unsettled by his father's death, that grief, especially when it was not properly tended, could turn even a reasonable human being hostile and confused. Maybe he needed to make an appointment with Dr. X for himself instead of taking down the appointments of others; surely there was an employee discount.

I read up on double exposure and grief. I read up on spirit photography. I tried to understand why my husband would not, or could not, see the boy in the tree even after I had made his presence known. Had his not-seeing been a charade or some kind of test? From the library I checked out *Chronicles of the Photographs of Spiritual Beings and Phenomena Invisible to the Material Eye*. Yet nothing provided an explanation as satisfying as the one I knew to be true the moment I saw the photograph—my husband had done something to that boy in the tree.

■ ■ ■

A great many people know the name Margaret Wise Brown, but how about Clement Hurd, who illustrated *Goodnight Moon* and studied with cubists in Paris? By the time my husband introduced his childhood photo into our lives, I'd had a very successful run of illustration projects, all with major publishers, though I had not won a Caldecott Medal. The things that hadn't happened, the honors not bestowed, had never bothered me earlier in my career, when time felt like a field without a visible horizon—but now that dark line had appeared in the distance and the story I had always told myself about my own limitless prospects was breaking down; *not yet* was starting to feel more like *not ever.*

That summer, the commission from the wealthy eccentric was my sole job. This happened on occasion, someone coming along with a vanity project and enough money to make it a real thing in the world. The author intended to self-publish the book and when I received the text it was like no children's book I had ever before seen—a story about a surrealist ballet troupe comprised of animals. Later the reader learned the troupe was being held captive by a terrible dictator, in an unnamed country. The animals, tired of dancing to *Ballet Mécanique*, longed for escape. At the end, a giraffe made a run for it and was shot dead by a firing squad. The wealthy eccentric had suggested I watch Jean Cocteau's dadaist ballet *Les Mariés de la Tour Eiffel* for inspiration. It was a bewildering experience. Halfway through, a lion galloped onto the stage and ate a dancer for breakfast.

I did not care for the ballet. The music set my nerves on edge—and I wasn't alone. When my husband heard *Les Mariés de la Tour Eiffel* emanating from my studio one Saturday, two weeks after he showed me the photo, he ran over and began pounding on the door. He was wearing his gardening gloves and brandishing a pair of shears. His own long-dead mother had been a dancer as a young woman, though I had always imagined her doing classical productions, like *The Nutcracker* or *Swan Lake.*

I put on my headphones and he retreated from the door. I sensed his comprehension of the world was becoming constricted in a way I did not yet understand.

I had no idea if the wealthy eccentric's story was intended to be a comment on authoritarian regimes or the privatization of art or the cruelty of keeping animals in captivity, but I felt certain no child would ever want to read it. To test my theory I waited one evening by the backyard fence until the neighbor's little boy came out to play.

"Have you ever heard of *Ballet Mécanique* or *Les Mariés de la Tour Eiffel*?" I asked the boy through the wood slats. "Do you know what a dictator is?"

The boy yelped and ran inside. Not long after, his mother called and demanded to know what was wrong with me, bringing up French words and dictators to an eight-year-old.

"You don't behave how people are supposed to," the mother huffed into the phone. Often children's book illustrators were assumed to have kind and whimsical natures—a foolish expectation, for all the best children's literature, if anyone has been paying attention, hinges on betrayal, the heartlessness of nature, death.

As it happened, my husband was adamantly against us having children, given what had happened to his own mother. He said that mothers terrified him and he would lose his mind if I ever became one. In the early years of our marriage, I'd had fantasies about testing the limits of his revulsion. If I handed him a forged pregnancy test, for example, would I turn fearsome and unrecognizable before his very eyes?

Despite the shortcomings in the wealthy eccentric's story, I had become quite fond of the animals themselves, given all the time I had spent coaxing them to life. To cope with the personal loss I anticipated feeling at the project's end, I decided to repaint the living room walls. I would leave paint samples scattered around the house and when my husband was home, I would make a big show of reviewing them, scrutinizing the difference between Shy Violet and Mountain Majesty. Really, though, the paint job was a cover-up for a secret plan.

That night, as I ate dinner alone at our kitchen island, I pictured my husband working after hours in Dr. X's office, filing paperwork in his gardening gloves, and finalized the details of my plot. First, I would blanket the living room floor in plastic sheeting and haul all the furniture into the center. I estimated it would take me two days to paint the walls and once the paint had dried, I planned to stencil a miniature version of each animal onto areas that would be covered once the furniture had been returned to its rightful place.

I was starting to feel like I was in need of reinforcements.

■　■　■

I never told my husband about the voicemails his dying father left me in the middle of the night. I suppose it was the way my father-in-law always called at a time when he knew he would not reach me and rambled on until my voicemail was full—the whole thing had the tone of a confessional.

In these messages, my father-in-law told me he had decided to limit his food intake to what was farmed in Florida, which amounted to consuming a great deal of citrus and sugarcane, sweet corn and boiled peanuts. He had regular sexual fantasies about the woman in the red uniform who rang a bell for the Salvation Army outside Walmart. He told me he visited Teotihuacán in the sixties—before he was married, before he was a father—and saved a French tourist from leaping to her death from the top of the sun pyramid. She had climbed all the way up there to die. Many years would pass before he heard the phrase "suicide tourism"—which struck him as such a rude plan, to travel to a different country for the express purpose of making a bloody mess. My father-in-law said he'd grabbed this French tourist by the shoulders and shook her so hard her sunglasses fell off her face and clattered down the side of the pyramid. "Look at all this beauty," he'd said. To my voicemail he confessed that he wouldn't know what to tell a suicidal person now, as an older man, nor did he know what had happened to the French tourist after they got down from the pyramid. Yet this was the only time he could say with any certainty that he'd helped save a life.

I wondered if he'd held on to this memory so tightly because he'd been unable to save his own wife. They were on their way to the hospital when the car broke down. She gave birth on the side of the road and then bled out in the backseat. Umbilical cord cut with pliers.

His final missive was just static and silence and then, right before the cutoff, he said: "Did I ever tell you about my other son?"

The first time I listened to the message, I felt like I was holding a cold stone in my mouth. After I played it again, I decided to chalk his words up to delirium, given that being in close contact with the end of all time could make a person behave very strangely. But when my husband showed me the photo, with the pale boy perched in the tree, the boy my husband refused to recognize, the boy that compelled him to burn and bury the evidence—well, the memory had returned like an avalanche.

Did I ever tell you about my other son?

▪ ▪ ▪

I decided to put the question to my husband directly. One morning, I poured him a coffee and pressed the mug into his gloved hands, the fingertips damp and dark from soil, and whispered, "Did I ever tell you about my other son?" I had spent many hours testing different shades of paint in the living room and by then the entire house reeked of chemicals.

He startled, sloshing coffee over the rim of the mug and onto the gleaming tips of his dress shoes. He began making wild accusations. He said that I didn't know what I was doing, that I was insisting on keeping a terrible story alive, and when I told him that he wasn't making sense, he slammed the mug down on the kitchen island, sloshing more coffee, and fled our house through the garage.

I refilled his mug and dropped a couple of ice cubes in, because that was how I took my coffee in the summertime. I followed a faint dirt trail from the kitchen to the garage, where the door was raised, the driveway empty. I stood barefoot on the concrete floor, wondering what to do next. Already the ice had melted into translucent slivers. I stared at the highest shelves, searching for a way to climb up and see what else could be discovered among my father-in-law's things, and that was when I realized that all the boxes were gone.

That night my husband did not come home. When he turned up the following day he claimed he had fallen asleep at the office, but he did the same thing the next night and before long he was coming home only to shower and change; he claimed Dr. X had never been so busy. I would watch him struggle to peel a banana in his gardening gloves and wonder how long it would take for his beloved roses to wither from inattention.

■   ■   ■

Alone more than usual, I was productive. I submitted my illustrations to the wealthy eccentric and then called her up, under the guise of wanting to ensure my work was satisfactory, when in fact I longed to ask why she had written the book in the first place. Did she have a particular child in mind for this story and if so was this child perhaps a bit *unusual*? She explained that she had not written the book for a child at all; rather the story was translated directly from a dream that had been plaguing her for years. Sometimes she was the bear. Sometimes she was the giraffe. Always she was the animal who attempted to flee and was shot dead on sight; she never learned her lesson. She thought that if she made the dream real it would lose its power over her.

"But I'm starting to think," she said before we got off the phone, "that I might have made a terrible mistake."

A few weeks later, after the paint had dried, I spent two afternoons stenciling animals on the walls: a galloping giraffe behind the TV, a bear in a tutu on a place that would be hidden by a corduroy armchair. Our living room was now their habitat. I made the bear look gentle and entreating—head tilted, one front paw raised—even though I knew it stood ready to rip out someone's throat. When my drawings were finished, I pushed all the furniture back into place.

"You can never be too careful," I said to the whiskered lion pacing behind the bell-shaped lampshade. "You can never be too sure."

I was about to start rolling up the plastic sheeting when I heard a car rumble into the driveway and then my husband was standing on the edge of the living room, holding a large cardboard book. I watched him survey the walls, now painted a color called Suave Mauve.

"You're home," I said, wiping sweat from my forehead.

He set the box on the plastic sheeting. He pulled at the edges of his gardening gloves, sinking his fingers deeper into the fabric.

"You've been working so hard." He rubbed the sheeting with the toe of his dress shoe. "Why don't you lie down?"

"Don't be sinister," I said. "What would Dr. X say?"

"Dr. X sent me away. He said that I was developing a filing compulsion and needed to take a vacation."

"Good," I said, nodding. "We can take one together."

"I did everything I could." His entire body seemed to deflate a little.

I told my husband that I had no idea what he was talking about, that I hadn't had any idea what he was talking about for some time now. In response, he brandished his car keys and sliced open the box, revealing a row of book spines. The wealthy eccentric had sent me copies. I went over to him and lifted one from the box. I turned the pages, showing off my fine drawings of the animals dancing the *Ballet Mécanique*.

When I got to the illustration of the firing squad taking aim at the giraffe, he pulled the book from my hands. He got down on one knee like he was proposing (when he asked me, years ago, we were in a swimming pool and we both came up for air at the same time, our faces shiny with water, and then he said, "How would you feel about doing this for the rest of your life?"). I

slipped off his gardening gloves, one at a time; his skin was soft
and pale from the lack of sunlight, his fingertips pruned.

"I'm serious about that vacation," I said to him. "We could
leave right now. We could drive and drive."

He squeezed my hands and asked if I wanted to go out to the
Pitch.

Behind the furniture the animals snorted and stomped.

I was raised in the desert and always appreciated the way its
landscape gives you a chance to see what's coming. In Florida,
dangers don't reveal themselves until it's too late. The alligator
lurking in the shallow pond, ready to devour your pet or your
child. The snake hidden in the underbrush. The riptide slicing
across that postcard-perfect Atlantic. Sinkholes. Encephalitis.
Brain-destroying bacteria that flourish in overheated lakes.
Quicksand.

In the car, my husband said that lately he had been thinking
about his childhood in North Florida, about the things that had
happened there. He had tried to stop doing so, but found he was
unable; before he sent my husband home, Dr. X had told him
that which cannot be forgotten must be confronted. I stared
down the endless gray line of the highway. The sky was clear; I
felt sunshine in my lungs. My husband's hands gleamed on the
steering wheel.

At the Pitch, I followed him out into a sea of darkening
green. I ducked under ropes of moss and mildewed branches.
I kept my eyes on my feet. I took high, careful steps.

"Do I know everything about you?" my husband asked as we
walked.

"Everything except my thoughts."

We went on for a while in silence, twigs snapping under our

feet. I considered the possibility that our thoughts were the most important thing to know, because they made up the stories we told ourselves about the world and our place in it, what was possible and what was sacred and what was forbidden.

"Also," I added, "your father left me voicemails in the middle of the night when he was dying."

Ahead I watched my husband nod, as though he had all along suspected treasonous communications between his father and me.

"He told me all kinds of things," I said.

My husband swatted away a branch. "Did he now."

I relayed the stories. The sexual fantasies about the woman from the Salvation Army. The French tourist from Teotihuacán and how he had saved her life with beauty. I was surprised by how much I had to say.

"My father did not have the first idea about how to save a life." His steps turned long and quick across the forest floor.

"Did I ever tell you about my other son?" I pressed. I thought it might be worth putting the question to him again in the outdoors, even as I sensed us skittering toward a place from which we would not easily return. "That's what he said to me, in his last message. He said that and then he died."

My husband stopped in front of a tree. A massive water hickory, with a gnarled, mossy trunk and powerful roots, arranged in a way that resembled the giant hands of a pianist: fingers suspended above the keys, curled in anticipation. I touched the trunk and was surprised at how warm and supple the wood felt, almost like skin. Something about this tree was terribly familiar.

"That photo I showed you was taken by our father," my husband said. "A month before my brother disappeared."

He told me that the first time he and his brother heard their mother's voice in the Pitch, they told themselves it was just the wind. They told themselves it was their own sadness. Their mother, though—she was persistent. *Little boys kill things and climb trees.* His brother started climbing tree after tree, determined to root out the source of the voice, and then one day he went up into this very tree and never came back down.

A police report was filed. A search party combed the woods. My father-in-law hadn't believed my husband's explanation of what happened. He suspected my husband had done something to his brother, disappeared him by accident or on purpose, and since he was not prepared to lose another child he decided they would simply never speak of the missing one again.

As I listened to my husband, all these years later, I wasn't sure what or who to believe. Conveniently he was the only survivor, leaving no one to contradict his story. My sneakers sank down into the forest muck. I looked around for a big stick that I could pick up in a hurry.

It took a long time for him to forget about his brother, but eventually he did. Or maybe *forget* was not the right word. His memory was like a faint scuttling beneath the floorboards of a house. It was like eating a sumptuous meal to the barely audible sound of animals being slaughtered in the backyard. He had worked very hard to convince himself that there had never been a brother at all, that his brother's short life had been nothing but a strange and dogged dream, and he thought he had succeeded in getting the story to turn dormant—that is, until I looked at the photo and sought out the little boy in the tree.

"Maybe if you weren't so ruthless." My husband wrung his gleaming hands. "Maybe then we wouldn't be out here."

I thought it was unfair for my husband to blame *me* for the bizarre state in which we currently found ourselves, but I kept that to myself. I did not have a good feeling about where we were heading. I spotted a stick the size of a club near my feet. I picked it up and held it like a batter.

He removed his tie and stepped out of his shoes. He cuffed his shirtsleeves.

I can still scarcely believe what happened next and maybe I shouldn't, and maybe you shouldn't either, not with the way I was waving that big stick around as my husband called me ruthless. Who was *I* to be trusted?

But I'll tell you anyway.

Right when I was thinking I might drop the stick and reach for him, to say that eventually he would make it through this period of grief or at least present a case for it being too early in our marriage to seriously consider murder, he slung his arms and legs around the tree trunk. He began to climb fast toward the top. I yanked the bottom of his pant leg; he shook me loose. I ran circles around the base like an agitated dog, yelping his name. I tried to climb after him, but kept sliding down the trunk—and the moment I found a nub to rest my foot on, something to help propel me upward, an inner voice commanded: *Stop.* So I stood back. I watched his white hands clutch and claw. I watched his toes find the wood knots, points on a map he'd never forgotten. Once he was in the dark bramble of the canopy his body vanished. I waited for a long time, well past nightfall, but he never came down.

I walked out of the Pitch and, in the years that followed, wrote and illustrated a book about a little boy whose dead mother communicates with him through a tree in the woods behind their house. She tells her sad son wise and soothing things. The book was a great success. Very popular with the freshly grieved.

This is a gentle lie, I did not tell the half-orphaned children in signing lines. *This tree wants nothing more than to destroy your life.* I marveled at the story I had gotten so many people to believe. And then one day I got a call from a number in New York City—at long last, I was told, I had won my prize.

VOLCANO HOUSE

I. THE BULLET

I went to Iceland to see a volcano. Instead the tour guide took us to Volcano House, where images of gushing lava and smoking craters played on a movie screen. My sister said it was almost as good as the real thing. This was in Reykjavik, on a broad street near the port. Outside I could smell the rot of fish and salt.

At Volcano House, we watched footage of Eyjafjallajökull. Rocks with tails of white smoke and red embers shot out of a black sky, arcing like fireworks. During a re-creation of the Heimaey eruption, we learned the occupants of the island smoldering before us escaped by boat. After the movie, we examined igneous rock—obsidian, basalt, mica—in glass cases. Some of the rocks were as large as a human head. I wanted to pick up one of those human-head-size rocks and roll it down the street or bash it against a wall. In the gift shop, glass vials of volcanic ash were available for purchase. I bought one. My sister did not.

■ ■ ■

My sister and I are twins, but not the identical kind. Still there is a sameness in the slope of our cheekbones, in the dark blue of our irises. "Like lake water," her husband, Pat, told us once.

■ ■ ■

On the twelfth of November, four months after Iceland, my sister is running in Baxter Woods, a nature preserve in Portland, Maine. On that same day a man named John Evans enters the preserve dressed as a jogger, in sweatpants and sneakers. Inside he opens fire with a Glock 17, killing seven people, wounding ten. He is apprehended by the police on Route 1, near Falmouth.

This is what Pat tells me when he calls from the trauma center. I'm still in bed when the phone rings. I sit up. The covers make a puddle at my waist. He tells me the bullet is lodged in her cerebellum. She is in a coma. In the background I hear the hospital intercom, the sound of some important person being paged. "Slow down," I tell him before I realize this moment, like a bullet, is not something that can be slowed down.

I drive five hours from upstate New York to Portland. I don't listen to music. The windows stay closed. I think about the quake in Pat's voice. About all those people cramming themselves into boats and rowing away from Heimaey, into the unknowable night. At the trauma center, I rush into the cool antiseptic air, down white hall after white hall, until I find Pat by a nurse's station, tall and spectral under the fluorescent lights.

■ ■ ■

Her body was found in the woods surrounding the trails, which meant she must have heard the gunshots before John Evans came for her, must have been trying to get away. She was wearing a hot pink windbreaker. In the hallway, Pat grabs onto my shoulder, his fingers digging into my sweater, and leans. We don't talk about how the bright color of her windbreaker likely made it easier for John Evans to see her through the trees.

When the doctor shows us the CT scan, the bullet looks like a tiny egg trapped in her skull.

■ ■ ■

In Portland, in my sister's condo, her usual mug—the one with a Snellen chart printed on the side, a gift from a patient—is still on the kitchen counter, the white bottom ringed with coffee. I've always thought of her as the anchor: predictable, stationary. A point on the map I could return to. Her datebook is open on the dining room table. I peer down at the entries done in careful red pen. All of a sudden I feel like an interloper.

"As long as you like," Pat says as he carries my backpack into the guest room. It's never been just the two of us before. I sit on the bed and think about how sometimes it was hard being her sister. If she was the anchor, being around her made me feel like air—transparent, insubstantial.

I do not feel like air when I see her now.

■ ■ ■

Our hotel in Iceland was called the Borg and it looked like a white castle. Some of the rooms—though not ours—overlooked Austurvöllur, a large park with a bronze statue in the center. It was July and at night we kept the draperies open, flooding our room with milky light. I felt like we were living inside a single continuous day, a day that would last forever, which made me feel like we would last forever too.

■ ■ ■

After a month in the trauma center and no improvement, she is moved to a long-term care facility in Augusta. She is awake, in the medical sense of the word, but she is not aware. She can breathe on her own, but she cannot talk. She cannot hear us talking to her. Tubes carry fluids in and out of her body. Without these tubes, she will die. Pat works in real estate and business is booming in Portland, the once sleepy port city now flooded with deep-pocketed buyers from Boston and Manhattan. In upstate New York, I work in a copy shop owned by two Russian brothers; I ask to cut my days and start going to Maine every week to help. Once in a while my sister opens her eyes, and we watch one deep blue iris drift up to the ceiling, the other toward the door.

■ ■ ■

I bring the vial of ash to her bedside. The glass is warm from the heat of my hands. "Do you remember?" I ask her. The walls are the color of canned peas. A window looks out on a desolate parking lot. Her right pinkie twitches on the thin white blanket. The ash smells like nothing. I bend down and massage a bit into her arm.

■ ■ ■

In the condo, Pat and I watch the local news, the eleven o'clock edition. "John Evans, John Evans," the reporters keep saying, and then we are startled to see our own faces on TV: a wavy image of us leaving the trauma center, heads bowed, arms around each other.

■ ■ ■

I start playing a game with my sister where I pretend she has telepathic powers.

"What am I thinking now?" I ask, out loud if we are alone, silently if Pat is there. Today, alone, I ask the question twice and watch for a reaction: a blink, a twitch. We have been encouraged to not read into these little movements.

"You're right, as usual. Of course I was thinking about the bay."

Imagine this: the three of us spilling from the condo late one night, wine-drunk. Two days before Iceland. We followed the sandy trail down to East End Beach. We decided to go into the water. It was too dark to see anything but shapes: swells of breast and belly, long lines of torso and leg. We left our clothes heaped in the sand.

My sister went in first. Pat followed. The moon dropped a net of light over the water, and I watched his high white ass disappear into the bay. Earlier I tried to explain to my sister how life felt like circling a giant dome, knocking and knocking on the smooth shell, searching for the door. Real life was happening in there, I was sure—if only I could find my way inside.

"Happiness is a choice," she said, and I hated her a little for talking like that.

In the bay, I caught up to my sister. I dove underwater, into the vast cold, and found her ankle. I wrapped my hand around it and squeezed.

"What's your problem?" she said when I surfaced. "You scared me half to death."

"Boo!" I said, splashing. "Look who still can't take a fucking joke."

"Break it up over there," said Pat.

II. THE MURDER ROOM

The day after Volcano House, we went to Thingvellir, a national park. For the first part of the drive, the guide regaled us with a ghost story about a deacon and his horse. The deacon was engaged to a woman who lived on the opposite side of a river and when he was riding over to see her one winter the ice broke and the deacon died. On Christmas Eve, his fiancée, not yet informed of the deacon's death, answered the door to find the deacon's horse and the deacon himself. Together they rode off and it wasn't until they were in the moonlight that she realized the deacon was a skeleton, his skull as bare and white as moon rock. The deacon stopped at a cemetery and attempted to drag his fiancée into an open grave, but she managed to escape to a church and was spared, or so she thought, because apparently the deacon's ghost continued to haunt her every day after, a matter that was resolved only with the help of a sorcerer.

"The deacon supports my theory that matrimony is a dangerous and antiquated institution," I told my sister after the story was over.

"If only you had warned me." She leaned into my shoulder and I smelled the lavender hair oil she'd used since college.

The bus passed through a town called Mosfellsbær, moving north.

"If we can travel an hour to see a park, I don't see why we can't visit a volcano," I said.

"Give it a rest," she replied. "That movie was pretty good."

The first time I read about Iceland, the landscape sounded so foreign: neighbor to the North Pole, night-washed winters, light-bleached summers. It seemed like a place that must be terribly far away, but the flight from New York took less time than flying to California.

I looked around at the other passengers. An older couple had fallen asleep, hands crumpled in their laps. A woman in a blue visor read a paperback mystery. A man studied a map of Iceland with intent. I felt a growing emptiness, spreading out inside me like a sea. I stared out at the passing landscape, startled by the absence of trees.

■ ■ ■

Every evening, my sister called Pat from our hotel room. I listened to her describe the tart Icelandic yogurt and the alien grace of the swans in Tjörnin Pond. Impressions she never thought to share with me. A sonogram photo of us nestled in the womb: the kiss of her translucent lips, our miniature fists, curled and touching—how to return to that place? I had suggested the trip, even though I knew I would need to ask my sister to cover most of my share, with the promise that I would pay her back, a promise we both understood I wouldn't be able to fulfill anytime soon. Still, I wanted to see if it was possible for us to learn to act like sisters, if the chemistry between us could be changed.

In Iceland, I was thirty-seven, right around the age when you start to feel a need to account for how you've been spending your life. I thought that if I couldn't have a spouse to call or a permanent address or a dedicated vocation, I could at least see a volcano.

■ ■ ■

At the visitor center, we watched a video on the history of Thingvellir. Next the guide brought us to a lookout, where we gazed at ragged lava cliffs, at rifts that cut through valleys like stone rivers, at a dark distant lake bordered by low mountains, the peaks fringed with snow.

After the lookout, we followed the guide to a steep footpath. She explained about the Mid-Atlantic Ridge, which ran the length of the ocean. Almannagjá was the North American border; the Heiðargjá fault, to the east, the Eurasian one. These tectonic borders were separating. Every year the distance between the faults grew larger.

"This land might be ancient, but it has never been more alive," the guide said. "It is changing all the time."

The path through the Almannagjá was bordered by hulking ridges. Damp green moss oozed from rough crevices. As we descended deeper, a fog rolled into the gorge. The path narrowed. Patches of white lichen turned luminescent. We passed a section where the rock was coated in a peculiar grass, gray and hair-like. The man walking beside me was recording our journey on a small camcorder.

"I've almost got it," he kept saying.

■ ■ ■

That summer, it seemed like planes were always going missing. A plane vanished into the Pacific two hours after departing from

Beijing. Found eventually, in pieces. A dozen planes disappeared from radars for twenty minutes in Canada. What was happening in the atmosphere? On the flight to Iceland, I got the window seat. The longer I watched the sky, the more each turbulent shudder felt like a prelude to a larger disturbance. My sister slept through everything. "Wake up," I would say if we were on that plane together now.

■ ■ ■

I pissed behind a mossy boulder. Too much coffee at the Borg, too much water on the bus. I tried to tell my sister where I was going, but I was walking behind her and the wind was thunderous and she wouldn't turn around. I squatted and felt the cool air against my thighs. I wiped with a crumpled paper napkin I dug up from my backpack.

When I returned to the path, the group was gone. A cold drizzle started. I continued down the Almannagjá. A red fox scrambled over the edge of the ridge. I touched a patch of lichen the color of egg yolk. I noticed indigo clusters of wildflowers and an orange weed, the branches as delicate as a finger of coral. The rain fell harder. I kept walking, my backpack raised over my head. I felt the ground tremble, heard the rush of water. Suddenly I remembered the guide telling us we could only go so far into the Almannagjá because recent earthquakes had caused fissures in the landscape, breaking the path. I imagined craters opening like wounds in the earth.

■ ■ ■

Alone with my sister, I recite facts about volcanoes. I checked out a book called *Eruption!* from the Portland Public Library, a book I know I will never return: it is now an artifact of the After. I tell her the Volcanic Explosivity Index runs from 0 to 8. A 3 is classified as a "Vulcanian." An 8 is an "Ultra-Plinian," which in plain English means Holy Shit. Volcanoes exist on the ocean floor. The largest known volcano is not on Earth, but on Mars. A volcano can go extinct.

■ ■ ■

An index for comas exists too.

■ ■ ■

The echo of voices, the crunch of footsteps. Distant yellow ponchos weaving through the mist. It was the tour group, moving toward the top of the path. Where had they come from? I trotted over and fell into line, hoping to avoid a reprimand from the guide. Everyone was calling out for something, but the wind made it impossible to understand. It always seemed to be windy in Iceland.

A yellow body spun around and there was my sister, her face damp with rain. My body went airy with relief. I smiled at her and said, "Ég þarf kaffi," the only bit of Icelandic I had learned. She grabbed my hand and raised it toward the sky. Her skin was wet and cold. "She's here," she shouted. "She's right here." The trail of bodies stopped and turned, the white beams of flashlights spilling down the path and over the edges of the Almannagjá.

We were quiet on the bus back to Reykjavik. We sat in sep-

arate rows. "I'm missing?" I'd cried after she filled me in. I'd
been away from the group for too long. There had been a panic,
a call placed to the visitor center, the start of a search. "You never
know what's going on," she'd shouted on the path. The man in
the row across from me was once again studying his map of
Iceland with the intensity of a person planning an invasion or an
escape.

■ ■ ■

After Thingvellir, the guide marched us from the Borg to Lau-
gavegur for a "rúntur." Of course, we were getting the tourist's
version, the one that sidestepped any chaos or mess. We sat in a
pub with a glossy oak bar and framed photos of large, handsome
ships on the walls. We drank expensive Icelandic beer.

"I still don't understand how you got so confused," my sister
said. "A search party and you weren't even missing! Wait until I
tell Pat." Already I could hear her on the phone, chattering away
like I wasn't even in the room.

When the guide announced it was time to go, I stayed
planted in my chair.

My sister checked her watch. "We leave for the whale watch
at seven tomorrow."

"A sitting cow starves. Isn't that what they say in Iceland?"
I was repeating a proverb mentioned during a tour of Árbær, an
open-air museum meant to re-create the old way of life in
Reykjavik. I thought the saying had to do with the importance
of initiative, of forward thinking, but truthfully I could no longer
recall the exact meaning. We were joined by Tom, the man who
was so preoccupied with the map on the bus and who possessed
a chilly beauty—a slim nose, a plump, sullen mouth—I was just

beginning to notice. The group left us. He spread his map out on the table. The southern edge of Iceland was stained with red jam.

Two more rounds, a change in scenery. I told my sister that she could go back to the Borg, that Tom and I would be just fine on our own, but she laughed and asked how she could trust me to navigate an unfamiliar city after what had happened at Thingvellir. The three of us tumbled into the gray stone streets, into the endless light. I couldn't see the sun, but the sky was radiant, like the sun had melted and now it was in every particle. People were wearing sunglasses, even though it was almost midnight. White seagulls circled overhead.

We found a bar with bright red walls and a disco ball suspended over the dance floor. Clear liquor in plastic cups, the rattle of ice. My sister's voice was rising. Pale tentacles of hair were stuck to her forehead. The anchor was being pulled up. The red walls of the bar made me want to call it the Murder Room.

From a dark corner, we watched the tangle of bodies on the dance floor. The disco ball caught fragmented reflections in the glass. Soon my sister vanished into the rush, hands above her head. She had a gift for boldness when the social moment demanded it. She was always the first to cannonball into the pool, to dance at a wedding. She could shed self-consciousness at will, whereas I could not dance at a wedding without narrating the moment: *Look! You are dancing now. Are you having fun? Is this what living is supposed to feel like?*

"I don't think you were lost at all," Tom said in the Murder Room. He leaned in close, hot breath on my cheek. "I think you wanted to ditch us."

"If only I was that good at making plans."

He laughed so hard his shoulders shook. I didn't understand.

My sister returned, her cheeks glowing. She gestured for my drink. A group of men in tight white T-shirts passed and I swallowed a cloud of cologne.

"Is this Boston?" I said.

"We're in Iceland." She held an ice cube between her lips, then swallowed.

"I meant the band." I plucked the drink from her hand.

"Fuck off. I'm not that confused."

The disco ball fell from the ceiling like a silver bomb. It shattered on the dance floor. Bright shards went flying. The music stayed on. A woman in a short purple dress limped away from the crowd. She was barefoot and screaming—I could tell from the way her mouth moved, though I couldn't hear her over the music—and leaving behind a dark trail of blood, a sliver of the disco ball sticking out of her calf like a plunged knife.

We ran away from the Murder Room and toward the harbor. We passed a flock of young women in huge pink sunglasses, bare arms shimmering with glitter. We ended up at a food stand, eating hot dogs made of sweet dark meat. Warm buns, mustard, fried onions on top. I reached into Tom's pocket and let my hand linger. I pulled out the map and told him to find us on it.

■ ■ ■

Things we will try to get my sister to wake: doctors injecting drugs to stimulate her brain. A music therapist pounding out scores on a portable electric piano in her room. The therapist wears cloth headbands and Crocs. She asks about my sister's favorite sounds and colors, and I am surprised by how little I have to offer. Sensory stimulation with a sound machine that plays ocean noises. Deep pressure touch stimulation with weighted blankets. We talk to her. I tell her stories about volcanoes and ghosts. We rub her feet and hands. The longer she stays asleep, the more the list of dangers grows: pressure sores, blood infections, collapsing lungs, swelling in the brain, never waking up.

▪ ▪ ▪

At the Borg, I left my sister in the elevator. I had hazy ideas about wanting to show off my freedom. I have spent so much time stuck between the hot pulse of need and performing needlessness. Where is that right middle? In Tom's room, I closed the curtains tight. I shed my clothes and lay down, waiting. When he appeared at the foot of the bed, naked, I pulled him closer. He gasped, tipped his head back. Soon he was rolling away, into a waterfall of shadow.

Later, I climbed into bed with my sister. She slept with her arms sprawled above her head like she was still on the dance floor. I smelled her lavender shampoo. I petted the rough skin on her elbow. I slept for a while, and when I woke, we were shaking. I hugged a pillow. The bed frame rattled against the floor. I told myself this was nothing but a dream, even though I was awake. I closed my eyes until the shaking stopped. Earthquakes were common in Iceland.

III. FORM AND GROUND

We brush my sister's hair. We file down her nails. We are astonished at the way the body continues to grow without the consent of the mind. We turn on the sound machine and listen to the waves. We drink the bitter hospital coffee. I watch Pat clutch his cup and think that I have never felt so close to another person before.

At my sister's bedside, I remember the deacon, a misogynist even from the grave, and I start reading up on the ghost stories of Maine. I tell her about the three-legged dog rumored to haunt a beach in Acton. The bridge in Rockport that's haunted by a Revolutionary soldier who got so drunk celebrating the American victory that he tumbled over. Tales of people who still retain a presence in the world even after they're dead.

I don't tell her about the more disturbing stories I uncover, the stories that make me turn to Pat and say, "This state is *fucked-up*," like the headless teenage ghost who was dismembered by her stepfather on Halloween and now haunts the Androscoggin Riverlands.

One afternoon I'm in the middle of a story when she makes a noise that sounds like drowning. Her body seizes under the sheets. A terrible gurgling rises from her throat; saliva bubbles between her lips like she has a cauldron inside her. In the parking lot, a car alarm is sounding. I scream for a nurse. Pat finds me in a bright hallway, clutching my knees. "She's okay," the nurse tells us a little while later, meaning: she is the same.

■　■　■

What I know about John Evans: white male, twenty-two, no criminal record. Student at Southern Maine Community College, reported to have a photographic memory. Only child, single, rented a basement apartment from a woman in South Deering. In the preserve, he wore orange foam earplugs, purchased at a sporting goods store near Pittston. His parents—who look small and bewildered on TV—are lifelong residents of Gorham. His father admits to taking his son hunting as a child.

John Evans has a pink, hook-shaped scar on his left cheek, acquired in a dirt bike accident two years before the shooting. In the media, brain damage is one theory, followed by undiagnosed mental illness, as some people will go to great pains to find another reason for John Evans's actions beyond a desire to inflict chaos and harm. Then an old girlfriend comes forward with domestic violence accusations and some people start saying *well there you go* and others take this new discovery as evidence that John Evans was disenfranchised by feminism and the alienating ways of modern life. I listen to all of it and I realize that I don't care about *why*. I just want John Evans and all his kind eradicated from this earth and at the same time I know it's not so easy, that such an eradication would be meaningless if we can't cut out the roots.

I remember my college boyfriend, who came from a hunting family, and how one Thanksgiving he took me into the woods of Pennsylvania to shoot. The gun was heavier than I had expected; I needed a strength I didn't know I had to keep the barrel aimed at the paper target taped to a tree trunk, to keep pulling the trigger as my boyfriend adjusted my stance. I remember the wild cracking of the bullets and how the sound traveled through my body like voltage and how I could, hours later, still smell the gun smoke in my hair.

More than once, I've wondered why the police didn't shoot John Evans on sight, how it is possible that he's still alive. I ask the question, even though I know the answer.

■   ■   ■

Reporters in bad suits keep stomping through Baxter Woods. News trucks are parked in Gorham and in South Deering. Cellophane bouquets of flowers appear inside the condo and in my sister's room. Her office sends a card with hundreds of scrunched signatures. Her patients collect a donation for the Brady Campaign. We come back from Augusta to find a ham on the doorstep, an unsigned card taped to the foil wrapping. SO SORRY, PRAYING, FOR YOU, the card says on the inside.

January brings a memorial in Baxter Woods. Hundreds of LED votives are arranged on the trails so for a night the forest floor glows an eerie gold. The candles make bands of light around the trees. The reporters are out with their camera crews and microphones. There is the same unearthly fog as there was in the Almannagjá, as though Iceland has followed us home. I grip Pat's arm. The light makes it look like a spaceship is landing.

■ ■ ■

At a little bar in upstate New York, between trips to Maine, the bartender asks me to tell him my story, and I describe the places I have lived. Eight cities in ten years. Many different jobs. Few possessions or attachments. I've had some drinks. I go on.

"You on the run from something?" the bartender asks.

"Yes," I say, without hesitating.

■ ■ ■

After the memorial, a blizzard. I can't drive back to New York. I call in sick to the copy shop. The owner shouts in Russian. I hang up. Maybe I'll never go back. Pat's office is just down the street, so he leaves me alone for the morning. In their bedroom,

I open the closet, where my sister's clothes still hang, waiting for a body to occupy them. I slip a midnight blue blouse over my T-shirt. I stroke the silk sleeves. I rub the gold buttons. I find a pair of opal earrings on the dresser, next to a photo of my sister and Pat. They are on a beach in southern Maine, smiling wide. I put the earrings on and am surprised by their weight. The bed is unmade. I get under the sheets.

■ ■ ■

How confusing to be the husband of a comatose woman, I sometimes think as we drive to Augusta, past the dark lakes and the tall green trees. What to do with desire, for one thing. Where to put it.

■ ■ ■

As winter descends, the pure shock of what has happened begins to lift. Our register for beauty returns. Fresh snow on cobblestone streets. Twilight over the bay. During another blizzard, we stay up watching black-and-white movies. Outside, the snowfall is so heavy it looks like someone has wrapped the city in a blanket. We discuss things that do not involve pressure-sore dressings or insurance policies or gun control marches or any of the terrible acronyms we have learned: PVS and DPTS and GCS. Instead, Pat teases me about having not bothered to learn Russian for my job.

"You really don't know a single word?"

"I keep trying to learn *how can I help you*, but it always comes out like I'm the one asking for help."

■ ■ ■

One night we go to Bubba's Sulky Lounge, where a wedding party has taken over the dance floor. Men in suits, ties undone, make a ring around a bride in her white dress. I take Pat's hand. I do not narrate. We join the circle. We pretend like we belong. On the walk home I have a terrible thought: what if some kind of transference is occurring and the closer my sister gets to becoming a ghost, the more I turn into something solid, something real.

■ ■ ■

Despite the careful dressings and the nurses turning her in bed, the pressure sores on her hips become infected. Antibiotics are added to her IV to avoid cellulitis. Her GCS score shows no improvement. In his drab office, the doctor tells us that she feels no pain, that if we wish to cease nutrients and fluids, she will slip away without suffering.

"It is up to you to decide," he says.

We are sitting across from the doctor in stiff black chairs. Pat shakes his head. My throat closes like a lock. On our way back to Portland, we discuss consulting the priest who visits the facility, not because we are religious, but because the decision we have been tasked with feels so far beyond what a person should get to decide. Pat pulls onto the side of the road. He hunches over the wheel, breathing fast. We are somewhere near Bath. The snow is marbled with dirt. Beyond the highway there's a little bald hill, a cluster of spindly trees. Pat turns off the ignition and gets out. I watch him scramble over the hill. I run after him, leaving the car behind.

"Hey," I say when I catch up to him. "Hey." He leans against a tree trunk. The bark looks charred. A wind shakes the branches. I find myself listening for the crack of a gun. I see my sister crouched behind a tree, darting from one position to the next, the careful crunch of the leaves. She is getting closer to the road, she is getting away, and then the walloping pressure in the back of her head, the obliterating darkness.

When we return, we find an old orange Corvette parked behind us. Two teenage boys in camo hunting jackets are standing by our trunk. The third boy is in the driver's seat, trying to hotwire the car.

"Hey," we shout, running toward them. "Hey."

A fury turns me electric. My throat unlocks. I move in a charge. I'm about to beat their hood, to kick their tires, but then I imagine one of the boys pulling a rifle from the backseat and aiming it at us.

"What were you doing out there? Sucking his cock?" the third boy shouts out the window before they drive off.

■ ■ ■

On a frozen night in March, Pat and I go to an opening at a gallery in Portland. The artist is my sister's college roommate. Apparently my sister never missed her local shows. At the gallery, the artist rushes over and takes my hands and squeezes. Her eyelashes are gooey with mascara. Red triangles hang from her ears.

"So you're the sister," she says.

I nod. "I'm the sister."

There is a video installation of a lighthouse on a cliff shot at different angles, at different times. Pat doesn't watch for long, but I am mesmerized. Sometimes the image includes water, sometimes a white road. Sometimes the lighthouse casts a shadow, sometimes it does not. The lighthouse takes on the appearance of being haunted. I think of evil deacons and three-legged dogs and missing heads.

"Form and ground," the artist says when I mention this effect to her later.

"Form and ground," I say the next time I see my sister, searching her face for recognition.

■ ■ ■

On our second night in Iceland, her voice woke me. She was on her back, in a tangle of sheets. A long, naked leg. The heave of her chest. "I missed my chance," she kept saying in her sleep.

IV. VOLCANO HOUSE

I missed the whale watch. I woke alone in her bed, my memory a smudge of light and sound. My tongue was sour. My bones ached. Bits of meat still wedged in my teeth. I caught up with the group at the restaurant listed in our itinerary for the farewell lunch. Next we were scheduled to visit Kringlan, a giant shopping mall that sold Icelandic souvenirs.

"Oh, dear," the guide said when I arrived. The group was seated at a long table, the guide at the head. Tom was across from her, his map of Iceland folded into a square on the table, my sister at the opposite end. "You missed, well, let's see, just about everything."

I plopped down in the empty chair next to my sister. The windows were open; I heard the caw of gulls. The man with the camcorder was showing footage to the people next to him. Soon waiters served us brown bowls filled with lamb soup.

"I hope you enjoyed yourself." My sister slurped a spoonful of soup. "I hope you enjoyed having sex with a stranger. I hope you enjoyed sleeping in."

"He's not a stranger!" I pushed my bowl away.

"You left me." She held up two fingers. "Two times you left me."

She had a point. I left her in Thingvellir. I left her in the elevator. Sisters were not supposed to leave each other behind. Even in Iceland I could not keep still. I wondered if she was calculating how much my half of the tour had cost her, if she was tempted to lean over and demand I pay up.

"How did it feel to be lost out there?" a voice said. We looked across the table. The man with the camcorder was pointing the lens at me.

There are people who diffuse and people who detonate, people who make a mistake and instead of fixing it they say: watch me be worse than you could have ever imagined. I put my elbows on the table. I smiled with teeth.

"I wasn't lost. I was looking for a Viking to fuck. I'm a huge slut. Just ask my sister."

She dropped her spoon on the table. A flush crept up her neck. Her jaw pulsed. For a moment, I thought she was going to hit me.

"Okay." She stopped. She raised a hand. I could tell she was trying to rein herself in, even as the flush spread to her ears. "You don't want to eat soup or go on a whale watch or stay with the group. So tell me. What do you want?"

The man kept filming us.

"Turn off that goddamn camera." My sister slapped the table.

I wanted to cheer. Again she looked at me. Again she asked. Everyone was staring, but I didn't care. I felt like we were on the edge of something honest.

"I want to see a volcano," I said.

■ ■ ■

"A true rúntur is not for the faint of heart," the guide told us after we announced our return to the hotel, pleading illness. At the Borg, we asked the man at the front desk if it was possible to see a volcano.

"Right now?" He rubbed his slender hands together. We nodded. He made a call, and within an hour we were driving a black jeep out of a rental lot. We departed Reykjavik to the south, on a road that hugged the coast. My sister was behind the wheel. I read directions aloud from my phone. We were bound for Eyjafjallajökull.

My sister tapped a fingernail against the window. "I remember when Eyjafjallajökull erupted. The ash clouds on the news. All those grounded flights. And no one could pronounce the volcano's name."

"The Internet says it's perfectly safe now," I said, even though I had not consulted my phone on the current state of Eyjafjallajökull. As the land turned rural, the black nose of the jeep dipped up and down. We swayed gently in our seats. The road led us to Thorvaldseyri Farm at the base of the volcano, a cluster of white buildings with red roofs surrounded by flat green fields. After the 2010 eruption and the subsequent recovery, the owners of the farm opened a visitor center. I lost cell reception and switched over to a brochure with a map on the back page. According to the brochure, the visitor center contained a gift shop and a small museum, where you could view an informational video.

"I am not watching another video," I said.

We ascended up a winding road. The jeep sloshed through streams and chugged across lava fields, where the green land was dappled with dark, pitted rock, as though something primordial was pushing its way through. Steam rose from the rocks, obscuring the view. I felt like we were journeying into outer space.

The jeep broke through the steam. The land around us turned silty and dark. I heard a rumbling coming from somewhere underground, like a storm was gathering on the inside of the earth. Smoke hissed from fissures. My sister paused, stared out the windshield.

"I don't think we should go any farther," she said.

I knew she was right, but still I grabbed at the door handle. I felt ready to jump out, to abandon her a third time, and then I felt ashamed. When she pressed on, I knew she was doing it for me.

Around the lava fields we must have taken a wrong turn, or missed the turn we were supposed to take, because soon we were bumping along off-road. We stopped to study the map. The earth shuddered again; this time I felt the windows vibrate.

"Did you hear that?" She spun the jeep back in the direction of the lava fields, knocking us around in our seats.

"I didn't hear anything," I said.

She stomped on the brake, pitching us forward. She rested her head on the wheel.

"We can't go back to the rental place," I said. "Not yet."

I had a different destination in mind.

■ ■ ■

At Volcano House, my sister and I sat in the front row and watched Eyjafjallajökull erupt on the screen. The real was unreachable, so we returned to the image. We were the only people in our row, which made it easy to pretend we were alone. We watched charcoal smoke flood a violet sky. We watched lava shoot through fissures. I imagined the burning heat of the earth.

At the apex of the Heimaey eruption, the lava sprays were tall as skyscrapers, thunderous. Onyx rock crumbled, as though the mountainsides were shedding, and revealed the red coal beneath. Smoke moved like water over the rises, toward the people escaping in boats. It looked like the earth was in the process of being remade.

The credits rolled. We did not move from our seats. We did not examine the rocks or buy more vials of ash. We stayed and watched the devastation all over again. My sister's hand lay on the armrest next to mine. The same long fingers, the same oval nails. And yet. In the morning, we flew home. At JFK, she had to change terminals for her connection, but I wasn't ready to let her go. I accompanied her onto the AirTrain. She stood, her suitcase wedged between her legs. In the next terminal, I watched an escalator carry her away. The anchor and the spinning top, destined to misunderstand each other. The next time I saw her, she was asleep.

V. THE CENTER

"You want us to *kill* her," Pat shouts halfway through another meeting with the doctor. He pounds the arms of the chair. Her brain is swelling; her GCS score has fallen further. We are silent on the drive home. At the condo, he throws out the flowers that have wilted, scrubs the vases furiously in the sink, sets them on the kitchen counter to dry. We sit on the floor and share a bottle of wine. Chairs are too civilized for our current state. I want to hide in the bedroom closet, wrapped in my sister's fine clothes. Overturned on the counter, the two pewter vases look like urns.

■ ■ ■

At midnight, we go to East End Beach, lit by a pearly moon. We strip naked and swim out into the bay. The worst of winter is over, but still the water is burning cold. Pat catches up to me, takes hold of my wrist. I turn to face him, my legs kicking, and I know in the night he has stopped seeing me. Oh, sloping cheekbones. Oh, lake-water-blue eyes. My skin tightens. My blood cools. I hear the low roar of a faraway boat. I feel the rippling wake. My foot brushes his shin. Who have we become while my sister has been asleep?

When it's time to go I can't find my shoes. They have been swallowed up by the night. I walk back to the condo barefoot, moving a little ahead of Pat, the cold stone stinging. The moon has gotten stuck in a wishbone of cloud.

I start talking about Iceland. The National Museum and the story about the evil deacon and his tormented fiancée and the Church of Hallgrímur and the tavern that served shark and puffin in little glass jars. My sister thought puffin tasted like chicken livers.

"I know." On the empty street his voice echoes. "She told me on the phone."

"What did she say about the trip when she got back?" On the sidewalk I track his shadow. "Did she tell you I got lost?"

"I can't talk about her right now," he says.

■ ■ ■

We go to bed in separate rooms. I stay up watching Eyjafjalla-jökull on YouTube. It is not the same as seeing it at Volcano House.

In the ancient times, Icelanders thought an erupting volcano meant the door to the underworld was being opened, that the sprays of lava were souls being dragged down to hell.

What does a volcano feel like after it erupts?

I hear a knock. I mute the volume on my laptop. It's coming from the space right above the headboard. I get on my knees. I press my ear against the wall, my damp hair darkening the paint.

■ ■ ■

In the morning, Pat wants to bring a conch shell to my sister. At dawn, he went for a walk and found it on the beach. When he looked up, he saw a white church on a distant hill, the spire rising through the trees, an aspect of the landscape he'd never noticed before. In the kitchen, he holds the shell as gently as you would an egg.

"Go alone this time." I haven't showered. I can smell the bay in my hair.

He looks up at the ceiling. I watch him swallow. Behind him the vases are still on the counter. "I can't. I can't stay in the room. Not when it's just the two of us." He turns the shell in his hands.

"She's so still. Her skin doesn't look human. Once I threw up in the trash can. I tried, but I can't. You know how. I've seen you. You talk to her. You know what to say."

I slide halfway down the wall. I don't mention that my topics of conversation are limited to ghosts and volcanoes, that I hadn't the first idea about what to tell the music therapist.

"What if I have to leave?" I ask. "What will happen then?"

"You leave all the time."

"But what if I have to leave for longer?"

He puts down the shell. He shows me his palms. "Don't leave."

My heels sink into the floor. My thighs tremble. I was wrong about the shock, I realize in the kitchen. It has not eased at all. Rather we have entered into a state of shock that will last for the rest of our lives.

■ ■ ■

We get in the car. We do not talk about the bay. An insistent wind pushes us around on the highway. I think of my sister driving the black rental jeep in Iceland, the shuddering, smoking earth. The shell rests in a cup holder. I do not tell him that last night I spent hours looking at tickets to Iceland. This time it will not be the season of endless sun. This time I will not go on a tour. At the airport I will get in a taxi and plead for a volcano. And what will stop me from diving right into the center?

Pat misses the exit for Augusta. He keeps driving. North. "You're going the wrong way," I tell him, but he doesn't answer. I smack the dashboard. I tell him to pull over, let me out, my sister is waiting, Iceland is waiting. He squeezes the steering wheel and accelerates.

We end up on Route 1, the same road John Evans drove down after he shot my sister and sixteen other people in the woods. The road curves along the coast. The car slows. I can see the water. The white clouds hovering on the horizon look like mountains. The shell rattles in the cup holder.

"Where are you taking us?" I ask. "Canada?"

He cracks his window, lets in a little air.

We end up at Gardner Lake, near Machias. From the small parking lot, I can see the dark velvet of lake water between the trees. We put down the windows. Pat opens the sunroof. I recline my seat and watch the gliding clouds. I smell the same rot that I once smelled on a street corner in Reykjavik, with my sister.

"Were you happy?" I ask, hands crossed over my chest. I never knew what to make of their married life. They met in college. They were in optometry and real estate. They went on vacation once a year. They had their own language of jokes and insults. They still held hands. I always told myself theirs was a life I could never want.

"Happy enough."

"Is there such a thing as enough?" I think of my sister talking in her sleep. What chance did she feel like she missed?

"Yes," Pat says. "There is."

■   ■   ■

I see her still body under the white sheets. The fluttering eyelashes. The skin as waxy as polished fruit. If you feel the back of her head, push your fingers through her hair, you can touch the place where the bullet burst in. The sound machine is on. Her room is oceanic. "I'll do better," I hear myself telling her. "Come back."

■ ■ ■

Pat picks up the shell. The outside is rough, but the interior has a beautiful pink sheen. I suspect he can sense me preparing to gather myself up, to move on like a storm. In this car he is hoping for a miracle. He tells me to sit up. He presses the conch against my ear, and I hear a dull echo. I imagine that echo growing into a roar and that roar filling me up or drowning me, I can't be sure what's going to happen.

He keeps the shell against my ear.

He says, "Do you hear it?"

He says, "The sea."

FRIENDS

Sarah had moved to a city of medium size, the worst size for making friends. A place is a place, she'd told herself upon arriving, but she had never before lived in a city of medium size. People were moderately friendly. The streets were moderately busy, the shops moderately expensive and moderately good-looking. She lived near a park with cannons and an American flag, the most patriotic park she'd ever seen. Beyond the park lay train tracks and a river of moderate width, slicing through the city like a silver vein.

Sarah was not a friendless person. She had plenty of friends, from cities large and small. In fact, some of these friends had offered to set her up with people they knew in this medium-size city. The site of her first friend date was a restaurant trying very hard to look like it belonged to someplace larger. Through a tall window Sarah spotted the prospective friend siting at the bar. She was sporty-beautiful, the kind of woman who could be glamorous in sweats because everything was of such fine quality. Sarah disliked her on sight. On the street she sent a text. *Sorry! Food poisoning!* The prospective friend texted back right away, with sympathy, and Sarah never replied.

On her second attempted friend date, Sarah, after two beers, started talking about her mother. Her mother had visited recently and insisted on staying in a hotel. It did not matter that Sarah, for the first time in her life, had rented an apartment with a guest room. It did not matter that she had promised to clean the bathroom and stock the fridge. Her mother had said that she did not feel safe staying with Sarah. Her own mother had said this! The bar was communist-themed. The second prospective friend shredded a cocktail napkin as Sarah rambled on, a mural of Lenin peering over her shoulder. Sarah went to the bathroom and when she returned, the friend made a hurried excuse about having forgotten to feed her cat, paid her share, and left.

The third friend suggested meeting in a park, this one neutral on the subject of patriotism. Odd, since they were getting together after work, and it was early spring and still cold, but then again she hadn't had much luck in indoor spaces. Aided by the small flashlight on her keychain, Sarah found this woman, Holly, sitting on a bench in a black gabardine trench coat.

"You found me," Holly said. "That's a good sign."

A sign of what exactly Sarah did not think to ask.

Before long she was once again recounting the story about her mother's visit. She knew this was off-putting to strangers but could not help herself—did not want to help herself, perhaps. Holly didn't leave or change the subject. Instead she said, "I can see your mother's side of things."

"You've never met my mother," Sarah said. "You don't know anything about us."

"All I need to know is what's right in front of me," Holly said with a shrug.

Sarah wanted to argue, but when she went to compile evidence to demonstrate that she was indeed a person others could feel safe with, she came up very short.

She and Holly continued seeing each other, always outside

and always at night. They played tennis at the courts by the library. They went for long runs along the river. By May Sarah had lost five pounds. "You're the perfect friend," Holly said once, in the moonlight. The statement struck Sarah as half-finished, like there was another piece Holly was holding back, but compliments rarely befell her and it felt ungracious to push for more.

One Saturday morning, Holly sent a text asking if Sarah wanted to meet at the train station. *Up for an adventure?* Sarah was pleased; spending time in the daylight seemed like a friend-promotion. On platform 6, she found Holly leaning against a concrete pillar in her trench, holding a round case by its Lucite handle. Sarah realized that she had been mistaken about the color of the trench—in the daytime it was not black and yet the exact color was hard to pin down, somewhere between eggplant and plum.

"I got us two tickets." She passed one to Sarah. The destination had been blotted out with black marker. Holly gave Sarah the window seat, and as the train chugged away from the medium-size city she pressed her palms to the glass and thought of the tiny cacti lined up in her windowsill—the plants favored by people who did not know how to take care of anything.

They rolled past Trenton, Philadelphia, Baltimore. They drank watery coffee and ate Babybels. When Sarah asked after their destination, Holly just said, "We have a ways to go." By the time they hit D.C. the sun was melting across the sky, bright and shapeless. Holly made another trip to the café car, and returned carrying a cardboard tray packed with little red wines and hummus cups. She handed the tray to Sarah and collected the round case. She said it was time to go to the roomette.

"This is an overnight?" Sarah said, frowning. She was not prepared to spend the night, on a train or anywhere else.

"We have a ways to go," Holly said again.

The roomette held bunk beds and the smallest toilet Sarah had ever seen. She sat on the bottom bunk. Holly joined her, unscrewed a little wine, and handed Sarah the bottle.

"That city was not of a good size," Holly said. "The people who built it should have stopped sooner or made more."

Sarah was troubled by the past tense, as though the city had ceased to exist upon their departure. She took a long drink.

"I was starting to get used to it," Sarah said, her throat burning a little. "The city seemed bigger at night."

"You won't miss it much," Holly replied.

The train swayed. Sarah felt the wine slosh in her stomach. "Are you *kidnapping* me?"

"Do you see a gun? Can a friend kidnap a friend?" Holly laughed and slugged her in the shoulder. "Seriously, though, I can't start over in a new place without a friend. Can you imagine?"

"Yes," Sarah said. "I can."

"You, my dear, are a cautionary tale." Holly loosened the belt on her trench and opened the round case, which was much deeper than it had appeared from the outside. She passed Sarah a set of thin white cotton pajamas, a travel-size toothbrush and toothpaste balanced on top.

"I should call my mother." By then the land around the tracks had gone dark and Sarah had killed the bottle.

"Forget about your mother," Holly said. "She doesn't want to hear from you."

In Hamlet, North Carolina, they climbed into the bunk beds. Sarah took the top, the ceiling so close she felt as though she'd been sealed inside a carapace. A little while later Holly's voice floated up from the floor.

"So what happened with your mother? I have my ideas, but I'd like to hear about it in your own words."

That winter, Sarah had moved in with her mother to help her recover from an operation, serious and invasive, and this arrangement had brought out the worst in both of them. Her mother had a little silver bell she rang every two minutes. All the ways Sarah tried to help were wrong. She got the wrong things at the grocery. She always forgot to refill the bedside water glass. She left the TV remote out of reach. One afternoon she locked her mother's door from the outside. She listened to the chiming bell. After thirty minutes, she unlocked the door. She claimed to have been out of earshot in the backyard, but they both knew. The next day she left a sandwich and a half glass of water at her mother's bedside, locked up, and went to see a movie.

"Let's just say things did not improve from there." Sarah thought it was close to midnight, though she couldn't be sure because her watch had stopped ticking in Cary. Her phone had died too, and none of the chargers in the roomette were working.

"Am I a terrible person?" Sarah asked.

"Yes," Holly said. "That's what makes you perfect."

Sarah asked Holly if she had brought a friend with her to the medium-size city—and, if so, what had become of this person. In response, Holly began to snore loudly.

Sarah supposed she would get her answer soon enough.

Next door a toilet flushed. Someone was having a sneezing fit. When she tried to remember the friend who had set her up with Holly, she failed to summon a name. But surely this person existed—otherwise how would they have found each other? She imagined this friend in the roomette next door, whispering through an air vent.

The next stop was called—Denmark, South Carolina.

Sarah rolled toward the wall. She listened for the voice of her friend, who she hoped would explain that while Holly had strange ideas about what constituted adventure she was really quite harmless. But that was not the voice she heard. Instead it was her mother, saying something about a bell.

KAROLINA

first saw Karolina outside the Sumesa on the corner of Avenidas Oaxaca and Álvaro Obregón. She was smoking a stubby cigarette, a sled-like backpack hitched to her shoulders. I stopped short, felt my heart lurch. Could it be? Karolina was my brother's ex-wife; they'd divorced five years ago, in Seattle, and I'd not seen her since. Right before their divorce, she had gone missing for fifteen days, an event still marked by dread and shame. The second time I saw her was by the bus stop on Avenida Michoacán. The third sighting was in Parque México, late at night. I had decided to walk back to the hotel from a work dinner in Roma Sur because I was having trouble sleeping and a long walk before bed—tracing the park's serpentine paths, imagining the alertness being drained from my body one step at a time—seemed like a preemptive strike against insomnia. The dog run was empty except for a young man throwing a tennis ball for a German shepherd. The owner was wearing sunglasses, despite the hour. I was just past the run, in the thick green center of the park, when I came upon Karolina asleep on a bench, squeezing her giant backpack like a lover.

The city was four months past the earthquake. The moment I had heard news of the disaster, I called my friend in the conservation department of the National Museum of Anthropology.

He and his family were safe, he said, though a building in their neighborhood had collapsed and thirty-two people had lost their lives. At home in Miami, as I watched the death toll tick up on my laptop, it had never occurred to me that Karolina had been in danger here too.

The man in sunglasses leashed the German shepherd and left the run. He whistled. The dog carried the tennis ball in his mouth. I have always been a little uneasy around dogs. I wondered where the man and his dog had been when the earth started to thrash under their feet, whether they had been afraid. I knelt by the bench. I touched Karolina's cheek. Her skin was sticky and cool. I grasped her shoulder. I willed her to open her eyes, but she seemed fast asleep.

"Karolina," I said.

My voice jolted her into the waking world. She stared, and then her mouth yawned open, exposing the sheen of molars, and she screamed. I fell backward, as though shoved. "Karolina," I said again, but she leaped to her feet and ran away, knees high, her giant backpack upright in her arms. I watched as she disappeared into the night.

A moment later, the man with the German shepherd burst through the darkness and rushed to my side. He took me by the arm and helped me up.

"Are you all right?" he asked in Spanish. "I heard a scream. Were you attacked?"

Had I been attacked? It nearly felt that way.

I was conversational in the Romance languages, as this was important for my work, so I lied and told the man that I had fallen, tripped over something in the dark.

He nodded and released my arm. I noticed him looking around, searching for whatever it was I had tripped over. His sunglasses were crooked on his face. The German shepherd paced around me—full of suspicion, I couldn't help but think—and then dropped the tennis ball at my feet.

■   ■   ■

In the wake of a natural disaster an art restorer—I worked for a museum in Miami; my specialty was mosaics—mourned not only the loss of life but the damage done to the history of human culture. I could not see an image of a collapsed building without worrying what had been destroyed inside. In the Great Earthquake of Lisbon, in 1755, the Ribeira Palace, which once sat on the Tagus River, was obliterated—sculptures and tapestries and paintings, by Rubens and Correggio, vanished. In 2010, the earthquake that devastated Haiti brought down the Cathédrale Sainte-Trinité and its famed religious murals; a painting by Guillaume Guillon-Lethière was believed to have been destroyed when the presidential palace collapsed. Years and years of artistic history—which is to say human history—gone.

Or nearly.

In some cases, people gathered the fragments and with these fragments made a new shape.

My husband (soon to be my ex-husband) was a psychologist who specialized in trauma; in this way, both our vocations placed us in close proximity to disaster and its aftermath.

■   ■   ■

The morning after I found Karolina in the park, I delivered a talk at a conference, on the restoration of Roman mosaics in the ancient city of Stobi. The conference had been on my calendar for many months, and the talk was one I had given before, and yet the subject matter felt freshly urgent. My throat was dry and I kept pausing for sips of water.

My friend at the National Museum of Anthropology attended my talk and though he was complimentary afterward he said that he couldn't help but notice that I had seemed nervous. *Are you sleeping? Are you feeling all right?*

Not really, I wanted to tell him, but it felt wrong to raise my own grievances after everything his city had been through. The major museums in Mexico City had weathered the earthquake relatively unscathed, though through conference chatter I had learned several smaller museums and galleries had suffered serious damage—a collapsed roof, a facade turned to rubble, shows suspended. The Permanencia Voluntaria film archive had been marred, perhaps beyond repair. A venerable gallery owner had died when her building collapsed in Roma Norte. My friend was involved with plans to help several badly damaged museums in Puebla.

After we finished talking I took a long walk, back toward my hotel. I walked through Jardín Pushkin, where children on Rollerblades were careening around an obstacle course of pink and purple cones; past tall apartment buildings with graffiti looping the ground floors and old women in bathrobes smoking on small balconies; past a man in an expensive-looking sweat suit grooming his black standard poodle on the edge of a grand fountain.

■ ■ ■

By the time I came to Mexico City, my brother was remarried and expecting his first child, and I was the one mired in separation. A few weeks after my husband left, I woke one morning forcefully in love with my friend from the National Museum. I started phoning him late at night, at a loss for what else to do. This caused difficulties with his wife, who my friend said could not be subjected to undue stress, and he told me that if we were to remain friends I had to stop, so I did, though the cessation of my calls only made my feelings for him firm into an unmovable stone, lodged somewhere between my ribs.

At the conference, I felt the ache of it each time I took a deep breath or stretched.

For as long as I'd known my husband, he had been proud of the fact that he'd remained friendly with all his ex-girlfriends; this was, to him, the ultimate mark of sophisticated manners. When he told me he was leaving me, he said he hoped we could remain friends. (In that same conversation he'd also said I was a dishonest person and incapable of change.) That day I'd remembered a couple in our circle who had divorced a few years prior and had somehow managed to remain companionable and the way my husband had spoken of them, admiringly, as though the transition they had undergone was the most desirable outcome for a marriage. Perhaps, with my friend, I was trying to reverse my husband's equation.

■ ■ ■

On the final day of the conference, I attended my friend's lecture on posthumous artist casts. It was an excellent talk, but when I stepped out of the hall the convention center was flooded with people, overwhelming. Plus, my friend had, over text, already declined my invitation to dinner, citing a need to return home as quickly as possible. A stab of disappointment, as I had hoped we could have a chance to speak alone. I left quickly and found an outdoor café in Condesa. I was sitting outside, under a cream umbrella, when I noticed Karolina crossing the street.

She stopped on a narrow concrete island near where several different streets intersected, a constellation of traffic, motorbikes whipping past. For a moment, I was frightened for her, but the longer I stared at Karolina the more the worry was replaced by a hot, churning anger. The fifteen days that Karolina had spent missing were the worst of my life. I now identified that period of time as the beginning of the end of my marriage.

Let me explain.

One evening, Karolina did not come home from her job at the health food store in Fremont. All her clothes still hung in her closet. Her alpaca scarf was on the coat hook, her necklace with the wooden beads was on the bedroom dresser, her striped socks were slung over the side of the laundry bin. I can be certain of these details because when I flew out to Seattle to be with my brother, he took me by the arm and led me around their house, pointing out her things. My brother did everything right: called her cell phone, which went straight to voicemail and was later found in a dumpster in the Central District; called her friends; filed a missing person report; organized a neighborhood search. Despite all this, within a few days he had been identified as a person of interest. It seemed the detectives assigned to the case had turned up a troubling call Karolina had placed to 911 a month before she vanished. Also, there had been complaints from the neighbors, fights so stormy they could be heard from across the street.

Before long, the detectives wanted to talk to me. As they asked their questions, I remembered my brother as a child, in our cramped apartment in DeLand. I saw him kneeling on the living room floor, clutching a tall glass of ice. I was splayed out

with a fever and longed for sleep, but my brother had heard on
TV that if a person was very sick, they must be kept awake. He
pinched a cube and rubbed cold circles on my cheeks. He did
this until our mother, who worked the graveyard shift as a cam-
pus security guard, came home. By then I had lost all feeling in
my face.

The detectives played the tape for me. I listened to Karolina
pant and cry, listened to her say that she had locked herself in
the bathroom and was afraid. I listened to my brother bang and
shout in the background. I told the detectives that never in my
life had my brother shown such aggression, even though there
were times when I gave him plenty of reason. I said his behavior
on the 911 call was an aberration, that it did not fit into a larger
pattern, though it occurred to me later that perhaps his behavior
did fit a larger pattern, just not one I was privy to.

"She must have done something," I said to the detectives.
"Something awful."

They didn't play the second call Karolina placed to 911 that
night, when she phoned a few minutes later to say the situation
was under control and no one needed to come out to the house
after all.

My husband flew to Seattle to attempt to talk sense into me
(his words). He refused to stay at my brother's house; instead he
checked into a hotel and insisted I pack my bags and join him.

"He is not a child," my husband said during those days of
terror and unknowing, in response to my attempts to offer up
evidence of my brother's goodness (most of which, I will admit,
lived in the distant past). "He is an adult and he has serious
problems. You've never been honest about him and look what's
happened. Now you need to think very carefully about what
you're willing to sacrifice for justice."

My husband was raised in a two-parent home, both his parents university professors, the kind of people whose offices my mother had been paid to guard, and still he felt he had the right to say this to me.

After that conversation, I, too, locked myself in the bathroom and wept, not because I was afraid of my husband but because I was afraid of what I might be called upon to do, the ways in which I might find myself unable.

The whole ordeal ended when Karolina surfaced on a friend's farm outside Vancouver, just long enough to file for divorce. She did not wind up in legal trouble, despite everything she had put us through and the resources that had been spent on the search; she claimed she'd had no choice but to flee in secret, that she had been scared for her life.

When Karolina turned up in Canada—I tell you, I have never felt such relief.

My husband was less reassured. The revelation that my brother did not disappear Karolina failed to satisfy him. The fact that he *could* have was damning enough. My husband had spent his career counseling trauma survivors—many of whom were women traumatized at the hands of violent men—and I told myself his work accounted for where his sympathies lay. Nevertheless, I knew my husband was disappointed in where my sympathies lay during those fifteen days in Seattle and beyond. All this disappointment was, I felt, intensified by the terrible movements in our world. There has never been a worse time to be a bystander, to be the person who says, *That was taken out of context*, or, *There are always two sides*, or, *We don't yet know the whole story*.

On the street, a white van swooshed past, and when I had a clear view of the intersection again, Karolina was gone from the concrete island. She had crossed over to my side of the street and was standing on the corner, staring at me. She started in my direction and before I knew it she was right in front of me, her tall body casting a long shadow on the sidewalk. Her hair was a thick blond rope, her eyes the same feline green. I flashed back to meeting her parents at the wedding—a small, reticent Nordic couple with whom, I understood, she was not close.

"I can't believe it," she said. "Of all the people."

She began unsnapping a mess of nylon straps, unshackling herself from her mammoth backpack and then propping it up against the café's concrete wall. The mesh pockets bulged with all manner of things: balled-up paper towels, a half-empty water bottle, a paperback, a garbage bag, a plastic comb. She pulled out the empty chair across from me, sat down, and stuck her arms into the umbrella shade.

Soon it became clear to me, in a way that it had not been in the park, that Karolina had not bathed in days—weeks, perhaps. She wore a long-sleeved cotton T-shirt and a denim jacket, the cuffs and elbows soiled. The skin on her cheeks looked pitted. Her nails were capped with black lines, her knuckles chapped, her eyebrows overgrown.

"Back in the park," Karolina said, "I thought I had finally fallen into a deep enough sleep to dream and wouldn't you know that I dreamed of that bitch who always hated me. But you weren't a dream at all, I'm sorry to say. You're sitting right here." She reached out and tapped my arm, as though to make sure.

"I'm no dream." I tried to picture where Karolina had been during the earthquake, in some trembling building or outside. "But I won't be staying long."

The server who had delivered my glass of white wine came by and stopped short, taken aback by Karolina's appearance, by her smell.

"Everything is fine," I told him. "We're old friends."

"Is that what we are?" Karolina said after he left.

"Look," I said. "I don't know what's going on, but why don't you come back to my hotel. You could take a shower, get something to eat."

"I could get something to eat right here." Karolina eyed my wine. "You could buy me whatever I wanted."

"I could," I said, without enthusiasm.

I was eager to hustle us out of public view. We weren't terribly far from the convention center, so perhaps I feared running into a colleague, more specifically my friend, and having to explain, even as I knew people were more likely to congregate at the bar in the Stanza Hotel or at the Gin Gin. Perhaps I had questions for Karolina that I felt should be asked only out of sight, behind a closed door.

"Is it nice?" she asked.

"Is what nice?"

"Your hotel."

I hadn't thought of how it would feel to escort Karolina through the glossed lobby, past the boisterous groups of young women in ankle boots and fedoras and black lipstick, and into the gleaming elevators. I considered the stories the hotel staff might invent for themselves as they watched: an idiot American taken in by a scam artist, a white savior hell-bent on tending to Mexico City's homeless, a feckless visitor enjoying the services of a prostitute. Or some other explanation entirely, though I didn't imagine they would include my having discovered my ex-sister-in-law in a state of homelessness or near-homelessness, unwashed and sleeping in parks.

"Of course it's nice," Karolina said. "You always liked nice things."

She gestured for my glass. I slid it across the table.

"My brother is well." I felt a prickling under my skin. "I thought you might want to know."

Like a sommelier, Karolina raised the glass toward the sky and squinted at the wine pooled in the bottom. She swirled it around and then killed the glass in one swallow.

"Does he still work for Alaska Air?"

I nodded. He had recently gotten a promotion, though I kept that to myself. I could tell her all about his life—his second marriage, the coming child—or I could say nothing, and my ability to grant or withhold information made me feel powerful.

■ ■ ■

I'm not sure what I want to say about my brother's relationship with Karolina, so I'll start with the facts.

They met on the Skykomish River. Karolina was a guide for a wilderness outfit that specialized in white-water rafting. My brother, recently relocated from Florida to Seattle for a middle-management job at Alaska Air, had been invited by his new colleagues on the rafting trip, some kind of trust-building exercise.

What they didn't tell him: they were rafting the wildest part of the river. (In time, he would learn that this was a stunt they always pulled when an East Coast person joined the team—so much for trust.) My brother would have been bounced right out of the boat were it not for Karolina—if she hadn't spotted his greenness before they even left land, if she hadn't shown him how to hold the paddle and explained the commands: lean in, high side.

They married six months after the Skykomish trip. My brother wanted very much to have a child with Karolina and he claimed that this disagreement—he wanted to, she did not—was at the root of their troubles.

A year into their marriage, she quit the guiding outfit, and after that her jobs included spending a season on a commercial fishing vessel; being a yoga instructor, a docent at the Center for Wooden Boats, an assistant at an herbalist school; selling antiquarian books. She felt it was unnatural to do the same old thing day after day. Whereas I always felt that there was something unsettled about her, the way she flitted from one activity to another—a quality that tested patience.

Two years into their marriage, I traveled to Seattle to give a university lecture on the use of solvents in tesserae restoration and stayed with my brother and Karolina. The afternoon I delivered my lecture, I returned to their house to find them screaming at each other in the backyard. Through the kitchen window, I saw my brother lunge at her, one hand outstretched like a claw, but then he stopped himself.

He stopped himself!

How could I be expected to believe the unbelievable thing when I myself had never witnessed it?

Three years into their marriage, they came to visit us in Miami. Early one morning, my husband and I were awoken by a commotion in the guest room, shouting followed by a loud crash, as if someone had thrown a chair or overturned a table. We lived in a town house with thin walls and I'm ashamed to admit that one of my first thoughts was whether our neighbors could hear. I did not maintain any kind of secret or criminal life in the literal sense—no gambling habit, no affairs—and yet I had always been dogged by the fear of being found out for a crime I did not realize I had committed, of my public self being stripped away and my unsightly heart revealed.

"We can't let this go on," my husband said. They had arrived in a rage, sniped at each other through meals and museum trips. We had been listening to them argue in the guest room for three days straight and I could not deny that my brother's voice was often the louder one.

"There is a line," I said as I got out of bed. "And if he ever crossed it, I would not hesitate to do something."

After Karolina went missing, my husband would remind me of this exchange and then inform me that what I'd really meant was that I didn't know how to address the situation with my brother, or else I knew it would cost me too much to try, and so I had stepped aside. I remember staring at my husband in our hotel room and wondering what it was like to always be so sure.

I found the front door of our town house flung open and Karolina running down the driveway. She wore pajamas printed with trout. She was barefoot, her hair wild, her thin arms tight around her torso. It was summer; the concrete had to be burning hot. She hooked a right at the end of our street, and I was seized briefly by the fantasy that this was the last time I would ever see her. My brother went out looking and brought her back a few hours later, both of them shamefaced, apologetic. He said he had found her at Coral Reef Park, her feet blistered and filthy.

In the final year of their marriage, Karolina called me at the museum, late one afternoon, something she had never done before. She said she needed to talk to me about my brother. She had questions she wanted to ask and she hoped I would answer honestly.

She wanted to know, for example, what he was like as a child. "As a child?" I repeated.

"Yes," she said. "Was he ever cruel?"

Cruel! I wanted to shout into the phone. *My brother* saved *me.*

Our mother loved us but worked long hours and was so exhausted by her labor that she could not do much in the way of mothering when she was home. It was my brother who poured cereal into my bowl, who bought milk and laundry detergent and toilet paper when we ran out, who taught me how to swim and ride a bike. I was petrified that one day he would disappear and I would be left alone in our small, sweltering apartment. Years later, when he moved across the country to Seattle, I, despite being a married woman with a thriving career, secretly hoped it wouldn't work out and he'd come back home.

During those fifteen days, my husband also said that my brother loved best what he felt he had dominion over, and couldn't I see that as a child I had been small and scared and easy to manage? His words had left me feeling both surprised and disappointed by how little he understood.

"What do you mean by cruel?" I'd asked her, standing up from my desk.

She paused. "Were you ever afraid of him?"

"Never." I shook my head for emphasis, even though I was alone in the room. "In fact, I don't know how I would have survived childhood without him."

"Thank you," she replied, and then hung up the phone.

■ ■ ■

"You were never this nice to me when I was married to your brother," Karolina said in the hotel room. The decor was simple and refined, everything done in silvery grays and soft creams, water in glass bottles on the nightstands. A rectangular window overlooked Avenida Veracruz. A hospital was nearby and sometimes I heard sirens.

"I'm worried about you," I said.

She stayed near the door, her hands slipped under the straps of her pack. I crossed the room to pull the gauzy drapes closed. Down below a family was waiting on the sidewalk, their faces covered in surgical masks to guard against the smog. A woman swept around them, working the sidewalk with a tall broom. I switched on the bedside lamps.

"That would be a true first," she said back.

After Karolina filed for divorce, I wrote an angry letter and mailed it to her attorney. I never got confirmation he had delivered it to her, but I could only assume he had. In the letter, I told her she had been reckless, that her disappearance had caused untold damage to my brother's reputation and his mental health and that, as a married person myself, I could attest to the fact that a problem in a relationship was like a great river of which both parties were tributaries. When was she going to take responsibility for her part?

"That was then." The room had double beds, and I sat on the edge of the one closest to the door. "This is now."

"It's easy to be nice to a stranger." She stared down at her boots. "It's even easier when you feel sorry for that stranger."

I started to tell her that we weren't strangers—we had once been family, after all—but then I stopped myself. I didn't know what we were now.

"Pity is a cheap emotion," she added. "It makes you feel superior when you're not."

"Don't worry," I said. "I don't feel as sorry for you as you might think."

Finally she slipped free of her backpack. She bent down and unlaced her boots; when she stepped out of them, the stench spread out into the room like a fog. Her socks were thick and a size too big, the excess material curling at her toes. She left her boots and her backpack in a heap by the door.

"Can I take a shower?" she asked. "It's been a while."

"Of course," I said.

She moved into the bathroom, almost on tiptoe. I imagined her taking in the white tile and the marble and the stainless steel fixtures, the tub as long and deep as a grave. The door clicked closed behind her; I heard the lock turn. The sound of the shower coming on. I knelt on the carpet and pressed my ear to the door. After a while, the shower stopped and the faucet started. A little splashing around and then quiet.

What I did next I'm not proud of, but at the time I felt— compelled. I crept over to Karolina's backpack and started rifling through the outside pockets. Everything had the same gummy texture as her skin when I'd touched her cheek in the park. Then, carefully, I unzipped the pack. I'm not sure what I was looking for, but I could not find anything beyond the tools for basic survival—packets of plastic forks and knives; a few dried-up baby wipes; a rain jacket; a collapsible bowl, the kind meant for camping.

An hour later, Karolina emerged swaddled in a white bath-robe, her hair dense and wet on her shoulders. I could see she had written something in steam on the bathroom mirror, though the letters were dripping too fast for me to make out the mes-sage. We lay down on the double beds. I was still fully clothed;

I hadn't even taken off my shoes. I listened to the tub drain and afterward, when the silence became too much, I turned on the TV, the volume low. The hotel got a few English channels, including Turner Classics. *Breathless* was on, about halfway to its bloody conclusion.

"How long have you been here?" I asked her.

"In Mexico City?" she said. "Or *here*?"

I took *here* to mean the streets.

"Either." I told myself I was prepared to listen to whatever she had to say.

■ ■ ■

Two years ago, after a run of bad luck, Karolina landed in Reno, a place she announced as the most depressing city in America, where people went to gamble and drink until they were ready to commit suicide. She took a casino job, the one upshot of which was a coworker, Francisco. When their shift ended at dawn, they would eat breakfast together at a diner called the Little Nugget. Francisco read detective novels on his breaks and in his wallet he carried a Polaroid of a floating garden in Xochimilco. When he showed her the photo for the first time, he promised to take her there. Before long, they were involved romantically.

When Francisco's work visa was about to expire he announced he was going back to Mexico City—would she come with him? Karolina had been to other places in Mexico—Oaxaca, Tulum— but never Mexico City. Over their breakfasts, he had told her about the parks with the soaring trees and the old woman in his sister's neighborhood who walked her Great Dane without a leash and the pollution and the endless traffic and the weather, arid and warm. He said she should take her time, think it over, but she did not need to do much thinking.

They moved into his sister's spare bedroom, in a blue-and-tan high-rise apartment building in Lindavista. The sister worked at a university; her husband owned a textile shop. They had two children, both school-age. Francisco began assisting his brother-in-law at the shop; meanwhile Karolina, jobless, had the days to herself. She rode the metro all around: line 3 to the markets in Coyoacán, 8 to the crush of Centro Histórico, 1 to the vast oasis of Chapultepec. She roamed the parks, the bookstores, the shopping malls. She got nosebleeds from the dry air. She learned Spanish from street signs and books and from the telenovelas she and Francisco watched on weekends. As her bearings and language skills improved, she took over some household errands—the grocery, the post office, where she was always attended to by the same clerk, a woman named Valentina, her face brightened by a thick coat of mauve lipstick. Karolina remembered the color because it looked meant for a woman twice Valentina's age.

After she divorced my brother, Karolina told me in the hotel room, she had worked to convince herself that she was destined to be alone. She brought out the worst in people. How else to explain that the man she had chosen to love wound up doing things that scared and hurt her? Yet with Francisco she permitted herself to wonder whether maybe she had just chosen the wrong person to love. If she made the right choice now, would she meet a different outcome?

For three months Francisco and Karolina worked to build a life together, and then the earthquake hit.

She would never forget the sound of the alarm slicing open the night—like a knife sliding across the throat of a slaughter pig, a violent unleashing. Everything was moving, each body a castaway on a wild sea. The bed that held her and Francisco flew across the room as though thrown by a giant. The frame struck a wall, the mattress hurled them onto the rippling floor. The kitchen cabinets flapped open and shut. The clock spun in circles on the wall, possessed. In the stairwell, as the residents stampeded down toward the street, the handrail shook so violently the base reared up from its concrete anchor. She and Francisco were side by side, but then he stopped to help a neighbor, an old woman who had fallen, and she got knocked ahead by the others, a tide of people that could not be paused.

Karolina made it out, along with Francisco's sister and the children, just before the building collapsed.

A white mist invaded the city. Entire buildings, entire blocks even, were reduced to tilting towers of debris. The night of the earthquake, civilians and military and medical teams worked alongside one another, hacking away at those towers. Karolina, barefoot and hyperventilating, had been handed a shovel by a stranger, a man in a surgical mask, and ordered to dig. The brother-in-law's body was found the day after, in the mewling light of morning. Three days later, Francisco's body was located by a search dog in white bootees and a camo vest.

The last time Karolina saw Francisco's sister was at an earthquake relief center. She was taking the children, traumatized by the loss of their father and uncle, to her parents in Guadalajara. Karolina walked out of the relief center with a blanket and a gallon jug of water and had been sleeping on the streets ever since.

She wasn't out there alone, as a great many people had been made homeless. One night, during her first week on the streets, Karolina came across Valentina, the clerk from the post office, her lips now bare, sleeping under a tarp with her teenage daughter.

■ ■ ■

As I listened to Karolina, I began to cry in silence, the tears oozing from the corners of my eyes and down the sides of my face. I hadn't expected her to tell me so much, to be so forthcoming. In the end, I was moved not by the harrowing turn Karolina's life had taken but rather by a sharp and sudden longing for my husband. It didn't take a doctor to tell that Karolina was likely suffering from some kind of PTSD, and my husband, the trauma specialist, would know what to say.

"Once I called you at your work and told you that I had questions and that I wanted you to answer honestly." Karolina rolled onto her side so she was facing me. "Do you remember?"

I wiped my eyes and turned to meet her gaze. I kept thinking that even though I had visited Mexico City a handful of times before I had never once been to Lindavista. "I remember," I said.

"Those answers, I guess they don't matter so much now."

"I guess not," I replied.

"But the thing is, you're right here. I'm wearing your bathrobe. I never could have imagined it." She shut her eyes for a moment and when she opened them, she said, "I want to know. Is your brother still angry?"

"How do you mean?"

Karolina flopped onto her back, her feet pointed at the starched white row of pillows. As she spoke, she jabbed a finger at the ceiling. "This is what I could never understand about you. Your brother was angry all the time, the angriest person I've ever known. You claimed to be so close to him and you never noticed? You're either lying or oblivious."

Intimacy could distort one's vantage, that much was true. Sometimes trying to see the whole of a person could be like describing a painting with your nose pressed to the canvas, though my husband would have argued that I hadn't wanted to see from a different angle, hadn't wanted to step back.

"What was he so angry about?" I asked her. "Since you're apparently the expert."

"About everything. About not being what he wanted to be."

"And what did he want to be?"

"A family man. Or that's what he thought, anyway."

"And you didn't want a family?"

"Not with someone like that."

Earlier, as I escorted Karolina to my hotel, I'd told myself she held information I still felt somehow entitled to, so that my understanding of my brother could become settled once more. But I knew in my heart that my understanding of my brother would never be settled again, no matter what Karolina said or didn't. I had known this ever since one late night in Seattle, when he took my hands and said, "You don't know what it was like living with her," and then, after a breath, "I'm so sorry"—and I had thought maybe my husband had been right, maybe my brother had done something unfathomable and unforgivable. Once you have a thought like that, there is no turning back, there is only pretending to. Really, in bringing Karolina to my hotel, I wanted to better understand how I had ended up where I had, and I could feel it coming now, that conversation, the answers I had sought and dreaded.

On the bed, my face went fever-hot. A sweat broke on my eyelids.

"Your brother believed life should be simpler for him," Karolina continued. "He didn't understand why being alive was so hard sometimes, he thought he didn't deserve that hardness, that he had earned his way out in childhood, so he was always looking for someone to blame. Me? I grew up in an angry home and I wasn't about to make another."

I thought of my brother's new, swollen-bellied wife. Had she ever been afraid? The one time I met her she'd struck me as affable and unambitious: an early-morning power walker, a drinker of decaf, a needlepoint enthusiast. Perhaps she was easier to manage.

"They played the 911 tape," I said. "The police. When they were looking for you."

Karolina pushed herself up on her elbows. "And you *still* wrote me that letter? After hearing what was on that tape?"

"It was hard to accept what I heard." I recalled a few of the letter's harshest lines and felt flattened by regret. "It was hard to believe that there wasn't an explanation. That there weren't two—"

"Fuck you." She kicked at the pillows, knocked one to the floor. "Here's your explanation."

That night, my brother had discovered that Karolina had been taking birth control pills in secret, after agreeing to start a family, and he had become enraged. He had punched a hole in the wall. He had grabbed her by the shoulders and shaken her. He had put his hands around her throat.

"But why did you call back, if you were so afraid?" I pressed. I could hear the pulse of a party swelling in a room somewhere above us. "Why did you tell the police not to come?"

"I wasn't ready," was all Karolina said.

I didn't know where to go from there. On TV, Jean-Paul

Belmondo was dying in the street and calling Jean a scumbag for turning him in to the police and Jean Seberg saying, *What's a scumbag?* Time felt epic, engulfing. How wou we bridge our remaining hours together, after such a tense exchange? I remembered there was a minibar in the hotel room and sat up in bed like a risen corpse.

"Drink?" I asked.

"How about room service?" Karolina lay flat on the bed. She pointed and flexed her feet, like a dancer getting in a good stretch.

I found the menu and brought it over to her. "Whatever you want."

From room service we ordered hamburgers and ice cream and we emptied the minibar, one sweet little bottle at a time. I tried to not think about the bill, which I most certainly would not be able to present to the museum for reimbursement. We began talking about subjects beyond my brother, which surprised me, since he was the only thing we'd ever had in common. Karolina told me about what she had learned in recent months: the art of sneaking into a movie theater in the afternoon lull, how to sleep so your pack won't get stolen in the night, how to not sleep at all, how to bathe like a large bird in a fountain. I told her I was getting a divorce and that I was in love with my friend from the National Museum of Anthropology, and Karolina, her eyes glazed, gripped my arm and told me that life was short and uncertain and that I should tell him how I felt. I relayed that I had tried, with my unwelcome phone calls, and she shrugged and said, "Love is suffering." I asked Karolina what she was going to do, how she was going to survive, and she hung her head and told me that she truly did not know. When I resolved to help her however I could, she looked up at me and said, "We'll see."

At a certain point I pulled back the drapes, expecting a twilight scene, and was startled to find pitch dark.

A little while later we were crawling around on the carpet, and Karolina went over to the room service plates, stacked high on a tray, and started dipping her fingertips in the little silver tins of ketchup. She held her hands up, so that I could see what she had done, then sucked the red from her skin, one finger at a time. I watched from the floor, mesmerized, and then Karolina was beside me, guiding my shoulders to the ground. She pressed her hands over my eyes, a blindfold made of hot skin. She pushed down hard, driving the heels of her hands into my cheekbones. Her fingers were sticky and smelled of sugar and tomatoes. I felt an immense pressure in my eye sockets.

"What are you doing?" I said, trying to squirm away.

"Goddamn," Karolina said, pressing harder.

This went on for another minute or so and then her hands flew back from my face and I was blinking up at the white ceiling, my mouth so dry I couldn't swallow.

"I'm tired," Karolina said. I sat up and watched her shake out her hands.

"That's okay," I said. "We can sleep."

"I didn't say I wanted to sleep."

We collapsed back onto the beds, and I started babbling about the first time I ever flew on a plane. I was with my brother and my mother and we were going out to Arizona, to see my grandmother, whom I had never met and who was dying. This was when there used to be phones in the backs of the seats and, during the flight, our mother let us call from the air, even though it was very expensive, just in case we didn't make it to Arizona in time. "Oh, my children!" my grandmother exclaimed when she answered, her voice small-sounding. When we told her where we were calling from—an airplane! forty thousand feet above the ground!—our grandmother made a whimpering noise and the line went silent. It wasn't until we arrived at her home that we learned that she had died in the middle of the call. Her sister rushed out of the house in a fury and told us that our grandmother was a rural woman and a religious woman and she had thought it was the devil on the other end, filling her head with lies.

I must have fallen asleep in the middle of telling the story or right after I finished. When I woke again, it was three in the morning and Karolina was leaning over me, shaking my arm and asking whether I could get her some toiletries from the front desk. The sash on her bathrobe had come loose and I could see the freckled tops of her breasts.

I sat up slowly. I felt like I was still in a dream. "Toiletries?"

"Some of those little toothpastes, those little soaps. Mouthwash would be good too. A hairbrush. A razor."

"Right now?" I squinted at the bedside clock and then at Karolina. My head was still clotted with booze, but her gaze was steady.

"They won't look at you the way they look at me. They know you belong here and they'll give you whatever you want."

It was that last sentence that drove me from bed. I padded down the hallway and into the elevator, the dream state slowly lifting. I told the man behind the front desk that I had forgotten my toiletry bag at home, and Karolina was right: he gave me what I asked for and more. I carried a plastic sack of toiletries into the elevator and when I got to our room, I found the door ajar, Karolina gone.

∎　∎　∎

My mother has been dead for almost ten years. Once her children were safely launched onto the shores of adulthood, she seemed to age in rapid motion. I don't know much about my father; he left before I was born. As a young woman, I used to entertain fantasies of stumbling upon him somewhere—a teller at a bank, the man taking my order from behind a bar. My brother has always claimed he doesn't remember our father either, that he was too young, though recently I've started to wonder whether he remembers more than he is willing to admit.

At the age of sixteen, my brother entered into a yearlong phase where he recited monologues, ones he told me he had learned from dreams. He would stand before me in the living room, already tall for his age, and I would sit on the floor and listen. The weather of his monologues made it understood that I should not interrupt him or leave the room until he was finished, but sometimes I felt surly and bored. If I wandered away to pee or to seek out a different form of entertainment, my brother would follow me from room to room. He would barge in and if I locked him out, he would bellow through the door.

I've seen things you people wouldn't believe.

They're crazy. It's like everything everywhere is going crazy so we don't go out anymore.

I bet that's how God hears the world: millions of sounds ascending at once and mixing in His ear to become an unending music, unimaginable to us!

Our mother was a lapsed Catholic and sometimes spoke in vague terms about angels and demons—I'd thought that maybe my brother, at sixteen, had become possessed. It would take me years to realize his monologues had all come from movies, memorized in secret, a pastime he had kept hidden from me.

Out of all the things I could tell you about my brother, this was the memory that surfaced as I walked the streets of Mexico City, looking for Karolina.

∎　∎　∎

I wish I could say my search was born purely of altruism, but as it happened Karolina had stolen my wallet. When we entered the hotel room together, at an hour that felt impossibly far from where I now stood, I had placed it carefully in a bedside drawer. Once I realized she was gone, I opened that drawer right away—shamed to be driven by my worst suspicions, but driven all the same—and found the wallet missing.

I cut across quiet streets. I detected none of the usual sounds—the sweeping, the roaring motorbikes, the canine toenails scratching at the concrete. I checked the benches, the bus stops. As I walked, I tried calling my husband, even though it was very late. What would he say if I told him I had found Karolina in Mexico City and we had spent the better part of a night together? He would be glad she was all right, I think—if sleeping on the streets could count as all right.

He did not answer. I wondered whether he was alone or with someone else.

I passed a small mountain of rubble, glinting under a streetlight. I passed a building missing its face.

I ended up back in Parque México, on those serpentine paths. Now that I was paying attention I saw many other homeless people—people lying on benches under heavy, soiled quilts; under garbage bags and plastic rain ponchos. No Karolina. As I approached the bench where I had found her sleeping, I spotted a wallet on the lip of the seat. I ran over and snatched it up: the wallet was mine and it was empty. Cash, cards, driver's license—all gone.

I caught my breath outside the dirt ring of the dog park, my hands resting on the cool metal gate. At first, I thought the run was vacant, but then a German shepherd with a tennis ball in his mouth shot out from behind a tree, a young man in sunglasses chasing after him. The dog ran circles around the park and then raced back to his owner, reared up, and slapped his heavy paws onto the young man's shoulders. They began to sway back and forth. What a pair! From the edge of the park, watching through a veil of shadow, it looked as though they were dancing.

■ ■ ■

I kept walking. I ended up in Hipódromo, on Calle Saltillo, which happened to be my friend's street. I had been there once before, for lunch, the last time I was in town for a conference—and perhaps I had walked by his address several times on this trip, hoping for a glimpse of his wife.

They lived in a two-story villa, painted blue with green trim, flowering vines curving over the doorway. I wasn't far from the building that had collapsed and killed thirty-two people, but their street was quiet and pristine. I wondered why earthquakes, unlike most other natural disasters, weren't given names. The villa was gated, with four tall windows facing the street, two on the first floor and two on the second. From the sidewalk I could see that the room I knew to be the bedroom was dark, but the second upstairs room, the one my friend used as an office, was, despite the late hour, still alight.

I stooped down and gathered a handful of tiny pebbles. I

pelted them at the lit-up window, one by one. I don't know what I was thinking. I didn't want to scream for my friend like a madwoman.

When my hand emptied, a woman in a white nightgown appeared in the window, spectral in the light's warm glow. She was very thin, with long hair that flowed down her shoulders, and there was something odd about her posture. For a moment, I thought she was standing with the support of a cane, but then I realized she was connected to a portable oxygen tank, the translucent tubes snaking across her face and down the front of her body. The picture came into swift and terrible focus: my friend's wife was very ill, likely awake because she was in too much pain to sleep. She had taken to roaming the house—slowly, dragging her oxygen tank behind her—to pass the hours.

I heard voices. The light in the bedroom flashed on. It would have been in the best interest of my dignity for me to steal away from the scene like a thief, but I could not. The whole situation felt like a thing I needed to face. When my friend came to the window, he put his arms around his wife and both of them stared down at me. While I can only imagine they were looking out in horror, from where I stood they appeared serene and beatific, like something out of a Renaissance painting, so lovely I could almost forget that my friend's wife might be dying and that he would probably never speak to me again. After a moment, they pulled shut the curtains and the room went dark, as they retreated deeper into their home, away from the fearsome thing that had emerged unbidden from the night.

YOUR SECOND WIFE

GIG ECONOMY

The photograph arrives in a padded manila envelope, pressed between two sheets of cardboard. The picture is a headshot, with the blue-nothing background of a corporate portrait. The dead wife wears a starched white blouse and a black jacket. Gray irises like slivers of ice; a modest, toothless smile; tasteful gold studs in her earlobes. Her name is—was—Beth Butler, and she was killed in a hiking accident five weeks ago.

As a grief freelancer, this is not the first time I have received such a photo, nor is it the first time the photo has been mailed with such care. The husbands (I have yet to be hired by a wife) contact me at a designated e-mail. I send them an online questionnaire and request a photograph be mailed to a P.O. box because I like to be able to hold the wives in my hands and, as my sister has pointed out many times before, I can't be giving these grieving husbands my home address. Next I require three videos of the wives in their natural environments: delivering a work presentation or jogging along a river or carrying a birthday cake into a crowded, singing room. Then I need a week to prepare and then we meet. Between impersonating dead wives, I work as a part-time dog walker and a part-time landscaper and a part-time food delivery courier. What an unbelievably exhausting moment to be alive, in this era of the gig economy.

THE OVERCOAT

I never meant to get into this line of work, though I cannot deny that I have always enjoyed being other people. In college, I interviewed to be a wealthy woman's personal assistant. Over lunch, she asked me if I knew the difference between *tortuous* and *torturous*, between *adverse* and *averse*. Once it was apparent that I did not, she told me that the ability to make these fine distinctions was a critical skill in a personal assistant and that I should not bother ordering dessert. It was late fall and the wealthy woman arrived wearing a magnificent fur coat, quarter-length and dyed lavender. When the woman went to the bathroom, she left her coat slung over the back of her chair and I walked out with it. I wore the lavender fur all through the winter and was transformed from a student who slept in the backs of lecture halls to one who made the dean's list. Every time I took a test, I imagined being a young woman of great means, of waking each morning to find my future rolled out before me, free of obstacle and horizon.

OLD PAL

I discovered my gift for impersonating dead wives quite by accident. It was the year after college and I dreamed of attending architecture school because I wanted to build skyscrapers. Then my best friend's wife died of a brain aneurysm and he did not leave his bed for a month. I was working part-time for a theater makeup artist and I brought in a photo of my best friend's dead wife and asked for her help. Three hours later, I turned up at his front door in a frosted-blond wig and tinted contacts and a prosthetic chin. I had even broken into his garage and gotten some of her clothes out of storage: a linen dress, strappy sandals, a black cross-body purse.

"Let's get going," I said when he answered the door. His clothes were rumpled, his breath rank. He was barefoot and his toenails had grown into small talons. "Or we'll miss the movie."

We strolled arm in arm to the theater, as I knew he and his wife used to do every Sunday. After the matinee, we had a drink on the patio of a nearby restaurant, as was their custom, and I ordered her drink, an Old Pal, even though I can't stand rye whiskey and so considered this flourish to be nothing less than an act of love.

"Forget about skyscrapers," my best friend said as I walked him home. "This right here is your calling."

Later, he told his grieving colleague about what I had done and then that colleague told a neighbor and then I had word of mouth and then I had cards for a business called YOUR SECOND WIFE. More photographs of dead wives came in the mail and suddenly I had four part-time jobs instead of three and was too busy to apply to architecture school; on the city streets I would gaze up at skyscrapers and wonder what had ever happened to the person who had wanted to build such great and terrible things.

MARCO POLO

Your Second Wife is two years old and my sister still thinks I'm a part-time prostitute. She lives in Australia and we communicate primarily through an app called Marco Polo. Most mornings, I wake to find a new video, usually filmed in her kitchen or in her bathroom, as she holds her toothbrush up like a saber. *I hope you're being careful*, she tells me. *I hope you're using protection.* Again and again I tell her: NO SEX OF ANY KIND is the first item on my contract and I only meet grieving husbands in public spaces. I once had to turn down a job because the husband told me his dead wife was agoraphobic and never left the house. I have binge-watched all the seasons of *Law & Order: SVU*, so I know what's out there. I'll give my sister this much, though: while I am not exchanging sex for money, my most lucrative asset has still turned out to be my body. After Your Second Wife hit the six-month mark, I felt awash in cash and treated myself to overdue dental work.

AUSTRALIA

Not long before I started Your Second Wife I visited my sister and her husband in Australia and had jet lag for twenty-seven days. One evening, I was sitting at their kitchen table reading *Pawsitive*, a book I had been directed to study if I wanted to continue my part-time job as a dog walker, while my sister and her husband cooked dinner. I kept getting distracted and looking out the window, to see if anything was happening in the alleyway below. I smelled chicken fat and balsamic. The clock ticked on the wall. The minute hand was five past the hour when I briefly became invisible. The window no longer held my reflection; I could not make out a body filling the chair. I picked up *Pawsitive*; in the glass pane the book levitated. I watched my sister and her husband stuff butter pats and rosemary twigs under the chicken skin, oblivious to the metaphysical marvel occurring in their home. I wondered if my condition was permanent and if so, if it could somehow become profitable. I was almost disappointed when the spell passed in less than a minute, like a fleeting headache, my reflection a pale flame in the window once more. My sister will tell you that this episode was merely a jet-lag-induced hallucination, but I believe it was a premonition, a sign.

THE CLAREMONT KILLER

On this morning's video, my sister says that the police have finally apprehended the Claremont Killer, who stalked the streets of Perth in the nineties. The police have released footage that shows one of the victims outside a hotel, waiting for a taxi. She nods at a man lurking on the edge of the frame; the camera changes its view and when it switches back to the hotel entrance the young woman is gone. My sister says that if you freeze the video, you can see the profile of the killer's face, sharp and bright, like the fin of a shark hunting a night ocean. Until his arrest, he was the president of the Perth Junior Athletics Club. Today is the day I am scheduled to meet Beth Butler's husband and I know this is my sister's way of telling me to be careful.

PART 3

Parts 1 and 2 of the online questionnaire are similar to what a person would find in an application for a mortgage, that is if lenders accepted applications from the deceased. Part 3 is where the husbands run into trouble. At this stage, sometimes one will tell me he can't complete part 3 and the job is canceled. This is because part 3 forces the husbands to get into what they would have rather not known about their wives or to confront how little they understood their private worlds. *What is the worst thing you ever suspected her of? When was the last time she burst into tears without explanation? What was her kink? Name all the ways she ever betrayed you. Comb through her remaining toiletries and send an itemized list. Did she use pads or tampons or a menstrual cup? What brand? How long did her cycles last? Did she ever bleed on the sheets?* Experience has taught me that nothing makes the husbands more uneasy than being interrogated about the menstrual cycles of their wives.

STOCKINGS

Beth Butler preferred Kotex tampons, the same brand she'd used since she was sixteen. Her lipstick colors were all classics: Lady Dangerous, Bruised Plum, Cherries in the Snow. Impersonating her will require a prosthetic nose, tinted contacts, highlights, and three teeth-whitening treatments, as Beth Butler had unbelievably white teeth. She was five foot eight, making it necessary for me to wear a kitten heel. From the video footage, I learn that, irrespective of occasion or season, Beth Butler always wore the same tacky black glitter stockings, the kind a teenage girl might slide into on prom night, in the name of festiveness.

WORLDS OF MYSTERY

When she was alive, Beth Butler loved visiting the planetarium. I meet her husband at the entrance, holding two tickets. "You're late," I say, because Beth Butler arrived early for everything and was thus always chiding people for running behind. I take his hand and together we sail through the planetarium's dark rooms. We sit in a theater and watch a video called *Moons: Worlds of Mystery.* The moons that orbit across the screen look like giant marbles. When one of the moons explodes, a child somewhere behind us cries out. I learn that exomoons are natural satellites, orbiting giant, alien planets, which I will admit I did not know before today. I can't claim that the gig economy doesn't ever teach me anything.

In the parking lot, I'm supposed to say, "I'm going to swing by the market and pick up clams for dinner"—Beth Butler's signature dish was linguine with clams—and then head to the T, where the train cars would be crowded at this time of day, but the husband breaks the script by asking if I need a ride home. The clouds move swiftly above our heads. My glitter stockings itch. I say the line about the clams and then spin around. My heels are clicking fast across the asphalt when a shadow looms behind me and a lunging hand presses a white cloth to my mouth.

THE GREAT BEYOND

I wake up in the dark trunk of a car, my wrists and ankles bound with rope, a square of duct tape over my mouth. I feel like my eardrums have been replaced by tiny bells. I can tell we are speeding across a highway, moving toward a destination unknown to me. I am starting to suspect that poor Beth Butler did not die in a hiking accident after all.

This is the problem with the gig economy, I think as I squirm around in the trunk. Everyone is so vulnerable and the rules for what constitutes civilized behavior—well, they're coming apart so quickly I've decided those rules were illusions all along. We have stopped seeing each other as people, as fellow travelers on this dying earth; we just see a gig or an economy. The men I deliver food to, the same ones who refuse to add a courier tip, offer me twenty bucks to come up to their apartments. The dogs I walk pull on their leashes and growl at birds and the owners send me angry texts, demanding to know why their dogs, despite all these walks, remain so wild. Once, in a recital hall, a husband pinched my nipple, as casual as can be, during a Shostakovich performance; his dead wife had counted String Quartet no. 3 among her favorites. The system is designed to keep us so depleted that we forget our sense of decency and become so mercenary about our own survival that we have nothing left to contribute to the common good.

The car slides off the highway and creeps down a road. I imagine metal streetlights and vacant parking lots and shuttered box stores. The car turns again, bumps down another road, lurches to a stop. I hear the engine cut. I hear the driver's door open and close. I make myself small in the trunk. I think of childhood, of little boys smashing snails with their fists. I wait for the trunk to pop open, but instead I hear his footfalls move farther and farther away.

In the early days of Your Second Wife, my sister sent me an online tutorial called *Uh-Oh, You've Been Kidnapped!* In a Marco Polo video, I called her paranoid, but in private I memorized the steps for escape. I grope the trunk's carpeted interior until I find the release. Beth Butler's husband is clearly an amateur as the release has not been tampered with. He's also failed to realize that once I shake off my kitten heels, the glitter stockings, made from a slippery material, will help me shed the rope from my ankles, as though Beth Butler herself has thrown me a lifeline from the Great Beyond.

I roll out of the trunk, feet first, my wrists still bound, my mouth taped. The car is parked on the glimmering edge of a lake. Beth Butler's husband has left the headlights on and ahead I can see him kneeling on the ground and unfurling a roll of plastic sheeting, probably part of some twisted ritual he lacks the skill to perfect. Woods rise up behind me like gravestones. Even in the dark, I know I have been here before.

WALDEN POND

Once I'm on the other side of the woods, I jog uphill on a quiet, two-lane road. On the shoulder, I pass a sign for Walden Pond and understand why the landscape looked so familiar. The last time I went to Walden Pond my best friend's wife was still alive. The day was hot and infested with flies. We ate tomato and cheddar sandwiches on the shore and then my friend and his wife took a nap under a giant tree. I walked the perimeter of the lake and when I returned I noticed, from the faint twitching of their mouths and the involuntary tapping of their index fingers, that they were having the same dream, like two dogs linked in sleep.

The sight of my best friend and his wife dreaming together left me feeling like I had never made a right choice in my life.

Because I've always been a little in love with my best friend. He moved to another city last year and we have now lost touch, as people do. Sometimes I wonder what might have happened if, during his time of grief, I had shown up at his door looking not like his dead wife but like my very own self. If I mistook kindness for cowardice. If I am just a person afraid to face the world unmasked.

Eventually I come upon a twenty-four-hour diner called Helen's Kitchen. The door chimes as I enter. The diner is empty except for two waitresses, standing behind the counter like strange twins, one on the left-hand side, the other on the right. They are both wearing forest-green aprons and holding white coffee carafes. They are wearing the same glasses, with pink cat-eye frames; their hair is pulled back into matching French braids. For a moment, I think Beth Butler's husband has murdered me after all and Helen's Kitchen is the afterlife. The woman on the left puts down her carafe. She walks over and rips the tape from my mouth.

"How can we help you?" she says.

I ask if Helen's Kitchen serves alcohol and the woman on the right disappears into the back and returns with a bottle of Fleischmann's and three little glasses. We sit in a booth, the two women across from me, and I realize both their name tags read HELEN. I ask them if they're *the* Helen and they tell me *the* Helen has been dead for fifty years, but every woman who works here is made to wear a name tag that says Helen. The first Helen, the one who stripped the tape from my mouth, points to an oil portrait of *the* Helen, on the wall above the entrance to the bathroom, and there it all is: the forest-green apron, the pink cat-eye glasses, the French braid. Everyone is impersonating somebody.

"Where did you come from?" the second Helen asks me. "And why are your teeth so white?"

"Walden Pond," I reply.

"I hope you didn't go swimming." The first Helen explains that a steady increase in swimmers peeing in the pond has given rise to a virulent algae that now makes those same swimmers violently ill.

"Life is just a circle of destruction," she adds, shaking her head.

The Helens pour us another round. I extend my arms across the table like a supplicant and they begin to work on the rope around my wrists.

"How did you escape?" the second Helen asks, and I wonder if she's asking because I came in with my wrists tied and my mouth taped or if because tonight is not the first time Beth Butler's husband has tried to murder a woman at Walden Pond.

"I've had a lot of different jobs," I explain. "I know how to do a lot of different things." I pause and add that I also have to credit my sister, the only person who has ever looked out for me.

PYTHAGOREAN IDENTITIES IN RADICAL FORM

These days I have apps that track everything—how many steps I take, how much water I drink, every cent I spend—but what

about the things that can't be quantified, like the difference between kindness and cowardice, or the meaning of life? When I
tell my sister about the incident with Beth Butler's husband, I
know she will plead with me to *get a real job*, but doesn't she
know real jobs barely exist anymore and not all of us are made
to run off to Australia? The longer you stay in the gig economy,
with its strange mix of volatility and freedom, the harder it is to
get out.

When I leave the Helens, it's four in the morning and the sky
looks like the interior of a vast cave. I walk to the commuter rail,
to catch a train back into the city. At the station, I pace circles
on the platform and think about how I will explain Your Second
Wife to the police, when I report Beth Butler's husband. Maybe
they'll think I'm really a prostitute and was about to get what I
deserved at Walden Pond. Either way Beth Butler's husband
seems like an altogether incompetent killer and I imagine he'll
be apprehended soon enough.

I peel off my prosthetic nose and leave it on a bench. I watch
the glowing green numbers change on the platform sign.

4:21. 4:24. 4:32.

I can barely remember the math I studied in college, back
when I still wanted to build skyscrapers, but sometimes the lingo
returns to me, like a language I can recall only in fragments.
Fractals. Pythagorean Identities in Radical Form. The Unit Circle as a pie chart for how I have spent my life and where that
time has gone. There is symmetry in math and there is grace.
There are rules and there are ways to circumvent the rules. There
is no chaos or rather chaos exists as a set of theories, designed to
help us navigate the most complex systems on earth. I remember
a line from one of my textbooks: *When the present determines the*

future, but the approximate present does not approximately determine the future. Translation: it's all about the initial conditions.

I consider my own initial conditions, all the way back to when my sister and I played hide-and-go-seek in the woods behind our childhood home. With my inborn gift for ventriloquism, I could make my voice leap from tree to clearing to creek, I could make my voice be where my body was not. I could adopt different characters, from the bits I picked up from TV or school. I was an attentive child; the world seemed like a bewildering place and I wanted all the knowledge I could come by. I believed that knowing the right thing at the right time could save a life. My sister always wanted to play this game even though it left her furious, but she is an optimist and she thought she could figure out my tricks. I agreed to play each and every time because I knew that she would never beat me, not so long as she remained uneducated in the art of being both everywhere and nowhere at all.

I HOLD A WOLF BY THE EARS

argot's destination is a walled medieval village several thousand feet above Trapani, overlooking Punta del Saraceno and the Mediterranean Sea. The village can be accessed only by a single road and as the taxi winds its way up through the arid copper hills, her phone chimes in her purse. It's her sister, Louise, calling from the airport in Rome.

"I'm not coming," she says, her voice dwarfed by the echo of gate announcements.

Louise is scheduled to attend a conference at the village's Galileo Foundation for Scientific Culture. Margot works for an environmental nonprofit in Minneapolis and hasn't been out of the country in years, but a month ago her sister's husband announced he was leaving and there came her invitation to Italy, all expenses paid.

"What are you talking about?" Margot hunches over, presses the phone tight to her ear. The taxi passes a sluggish van on a blind turn; she's thrown into the passenger door. There is no guardrail and for a moment it looks as though the driver is speeding them straight over a cliff.

Louise is a theoretical physicist. She studies quantum entanglements, particles that remained connected despite being separated by billions of light-years; she has spent her adult life, quite literally, on a different plane of existence, far from the world's savage rot.

"I'm going," Louise begins.

"*We're* going," Margot interrupts.

"I'm going to—"

The call drops, or Louise hangs up, before she finishes. Margot looks out the window and is startled to see that the taxi has completed its ascent and is now puttering through the village, the cobblestone streets curiously empty. She glimpses a piazza, a scattering of unoccupied café tables with navy umbrellas, a lotto, a stone church. The sky looks alarmingly low and then she realizes she's not seeing sky at all but a descending fog.

At the hotel, the lobby is empty. A man named Filippo checks her in. He's wearing a red polo shirt and jeans and a silver watch, a little too tight on his wrist; he has an impatient manner about him, a darting gaze. Margot gives Louise's name, since her sister is the one who made the arrangements, and makes brief mention of her traveling companion having been delayed. Filippo requests possession of Margot's passport. He needs to make a photocopy for their records, but at the moment the machine is broken.

"It will be fixed soon." He drops her passport into a large leather envelope that looks like a purse, without even checking her information, just as well since the photo was taken in front of a bright white backdrop in some remote corner of a drugstore, in the terrible afterlife of a hangover. She watches him stow the envelope under the desk and thinks about how happy she would be to leave the woman in that picture behind.

The automatic doors gust open and a giant white dog gallops out of the fog. The dog lopes into the tiled breakfast area, toward a table with carafes of coffee and a platter of tan cookies. Filippo grabs a newspaper and chases the dog back outside, but not before the animal rears up in front of the table and snatches a cookie from the platter.

"No one around here eats better than the strays." Filippo shakes the newspaper.

On the front desk, Margot notices a sign, a sheet of paper crooked in a frame, stating that tomorrow the road will be closed to accommodate the annual Time Trial of Modern and Historic Cars. The only way to leave the village will be by funicular.

"A race?" She remembers the steep climb to the village, the absence of a guardrail. "On these roads?"

"The Annual Enemy of the Restaurateurs is more like it," Filippo replies. Apparently the road closure prevents tour buses from journeying up to the village and depositing their lunch-and-souvenir-hungry passengers into the streets.

"Is that why everything looks so quiet?"

He nods, adding that they're also nearing the end of the tourist season. In October, a month from now, the hotel will shutter for the winter and the staff will have to find new jobs.

"And what will you do then?" Margot asks him.

"This and that," Filippo says with a shrug.

He hands her a walking map. He tells her to deal with him alone because he is the only one at the hotel who speaks English. She climbs three flights of stairs to her room, where the twin beds are low and hard and the shower floods and there is the most spectacular view she has ever seen. The fog has thinned and a small balcony looks out onto Punta del Saraceno, a blue hulk in the dusk, and the sea beyond. Wheat-colored hillsides, the valleys flecked with gold. Headlights porpoise along the roads.

She tries Louise again, but her phone is switched off. She leaves a message and works hard to not let her anger break through. "I'm looking at the sea," she says to the voicemail. "It's beautiful here. Like heart-stopping, fairy-tale beautiful. Come."

Margot showers, ankle-deep in standing water, and then puts on a loose linen dress and a sweater. At the front desk, Filippo is having a hushed phone conversation; when he sees Margot coming down the stairs, he turns away, the cord winding around his waist, and speaks faster in Italian. Margot steps out into the evening, and she cannot remember the last time she walked streets so quiet. She notices plastic compartments embedded in the time-blasted stone walls, each housing an offering to a different saint. She looks up and finds the Virgin Mary entombed in an archway, her plastic case framed by electric blue lights. The great white dog, the cookie thief from the hotel, appears from around a corner and trots beside her for a little while. She reaches for one of his silky ears and he darts away, down stone steps sloping in the direction of the sea.

In a piazza, she sits outside even though the air is chilly enough to make the hair on her arms go stiff, because she is in Italy and she has never been to Italy before and she wants to take in the sights, even if the sights presently include only a bakery and a freestanding bankomat. She is the restaurant's sole patron. She orders a glass of wine and a plate of sardines. She eats too quickly, anxious about Louise's whereabouts and what exactly her responsibilities are in such a situation. She hopes her sister just needs a night to get drunk on her own in Rome.

After she settles her bill, she tries to withdraw cash from the bankomat. Halfway through her transaction, the machine makes a terrible crunching sound and the screen goes dark and her debit card doesn't come out. She jabs all the buttons, but nothing happens. Her wallet contains thirty euros and two overextended credit cards. A pressure builds around her mouth, under her eyes.

"You cunt," she says to the bankomat.

She tries to call Louise once more, standing out in the cold as her sister's phone rings and rings. This time, she does not leave a message.

On her way back to the hotel, she happens upon the Galileo Foundation for Scientific Culture. The foundation catches her attention at first because it is one of the few places in the village that appears to be open: a gold cone of light beams down on the heavy doorway, the wood studded with brass nubs, and the oval sign hanging over it. From the shadows, she watches the door swing open; a man in a dark suit and glasses steps into the gold cone. He ushers a couple in from the streets, speaking to them warmly in Italian. Margot glimpses people milling around in an illuminated room, open-mouthed and lifting glasses of wine. She smooths her hair, her dress, and approaches the man. She looks very much like her sister—the same height, the same wavy nut-colored hair, the same pointed chin—even as they are not identical (Margot has bigger feet, a tiny bump on the bridge of her nose). She will carry forward the plan that sprung upon her a moment ago and if he has met Louise before, if he refuses her claim, she will simply disappear into the night.

She extends her hand toward him and offers her sister's name.

"Professor Allaway." He clasps her hand. His skin is soft and warm. "Piacere."

Inside she finds a table with laminated name tags. She picks up her sister's and pins it to her sweater. She imagines Louise wandering the streets of Rome, no idea that Margot is currently roaming this reception under her good name. She eats fat green olives and salty cubes of cheese. She drinks three glasses of wine—even though, on the tarmac in Minneapolis, she promised herself she would not have more than two a night. Two and she is still herself. Two is civilized.

When she notices a man in a navy blue jacket staring at her from across the room, she hurries down a long hallway, vaguely in search of a bathroom. She makes a left, dead-ending into a dim corridor with an oil painting of green hillsides dotted with white sheep. There are other figures—a shepherd, an angel, she isn't quite sure—in the background, but not enough light to see the entire scene clearly.

She hears footsteps racing up behind her and then a thick, starched cloth is bound around her eyes.

"Louise," a man's voice says. He has an American accent. He pulls the cloth tighter. He presses her to a wall. Her lips touch the cold stone. The man's voice is right in her ear, his breath a blaze on her neck. "I've been trying to find you all night."

The cloth falls away and she spins around. She can see the painting, the grazing sheep, over the man's shoulder. He is holding a white linen napkin. He squints at her face and then at her name tag. His eyes are bloodshot, watering. He is very drunk.

"Louise," he says again, as though he is trying to convince himself.

He slumps against her. She feels his erection through his dress pants. She has been celibate for the last six months, as part of an attempt to bring about a sense of spiritual well-being. This attempt followed a string of unfortunate one-night stands, culminating in a tryst with a man who worked for the Minneapolis chapter of the Sierra Club; she woke to him urinating in her potted philodendron and thought, *I have got to change my life.* She planned to quit drinking and dairy too, but had only managed to stay away from alcohol for two weeks, cheese for a month. She even went to a few meetings for the former and found herself disgusted by all that open, ravenous seeking, by the woman who stood up and spoke about how she believed in the basic goodness of human beings before going on to share that she had been raped while in rehab and that her ex-husband used to beat her with a tire iron. All those awful speeches, it was like watching a person who had been buried alive thinking they could talk or pray their way out. Optimism had never felt more deranged. *We're disgusting and stupid and weak*, Margot had thought more than once, as she looked around that badly lit room. *Let us suffocate under the earth. Let us all go extinct.*

"Louise," the man breathes into her hair, a little more sure this time, wanting to be. He begins to kiss her neck and she lets a hand drift across the back of his head. Her tongue is a stone in her mouth. Her arms feel heavy.

"Here?" he says, and she moves her head, not quite a nod but a gesture he takes as acquiescence. She tells herself that this is not her body but her sister's, that she can be Louise for a little while longer.

The man unzips his pants. His hand dives under her linen dress, she feels his heavy fingers shoving aside her underwear, and then it is happening and then it is over.

After he zips up, he blots her forehead with the white linen napkin, which he has held on to the entire time. He says her sister's name again, slurring the *s*, and then he takes a step back.

"Hey," he says. "Wait."

Without a word Margot gathers herself and slips down the hallway and out a back exit, the illuminated red sign a jolt of modernness in the otherwise archaic-seeming foundation. She emerges into a shadowed street, lights made milky by fog. She discards her sister's name tag into a trash bin.

This is part of Margot's problem, the way she can roll along for months and then be party to something so wholly fucked-up her sense of self is unsettled for a long time after, leaving her afraid of her own company, her own thoughts. Last winter, she went out walking in the middle of the night, for no reason that she could recall, and when the world came back into focus she was standing on the Stone Arch Bridge at sunrise, in a freezing wind, her lip split from the cold, her hands gloveless, knuckles skinned. She seemed to remember talking to people all through the night, there were so many people, but she had no recollection of whom she had spoken to or what had been said. And later, even though she had bathed and put on clean clothes and eaten a shriveled orange, her colleagues at the environmental nonprofit appeared vaguely alarmed by her presence when she reported to work. She kept thinking that she must have had some kind of look in her eye.

At the hotel, Filippo is still at the front desk, playing a game on his cell phone. The lights are bright in the lobby and she can see the bruised skin under his eyes, the tiny broken blood vessels around his nose. He looks very tried. She explains about the bankomat and her lost debit card—does he have any idea what she should do?

"Your card made a tasty meal," Filippo says without glancing up from his phone.

"I'm sorry?" It occurs to Margot right then that she has yet to cross paths with another guest in the hotel. "Did you just say tasty?"

"Call your bank tomorrow." He yawns wide. "They will figure you out."

■ ■ ■

That summer, Minneapolis was haunted by a man who slapped women in the face in public. He did it outside the Franklin Ave. light-rail station and the Walker and the Soap Factory. Two women on Hennepin, less than a week between them. He would rush up to a woman, slap her with an open hand, and then run away. It took the police six weeks to find him. The fact that he did not stick to one neighborhood made it harder, they said; also he dressed like a jogger to make his running less conspicuous. For a time it felt to Margot like the slapper owned the city.

At the environmental nonprofit, some of Margot's coworkers felt the fact of the slap made the situation worse.

"It's humiliating to be slapped," said Kiara, one afternoon in the break room. "Just fucking punch me in the face already."

Emma, meanwhile, had enrolled in self-defense classes. Bianca had taken up with a neighborhood watch group comprised entirely of women.

"I dare him to come to our street," Bianca said.

Two weeks later, the slapper would get Emma outside a bus stop. She'd planned to poke him in the eyes and then palm strike his nose, but when she saw that wide, flat hand take flight her arms stayed stuck to her sides. On the news, Margot would hear another terrible story about a woman who, as the image of a charging man swelled in her periphery, shoved her girlfriend into his path. It wouldn't be enough for the slapper to terrorize women; he would make them turn on each other too.

On Margot's walk to work, a route that left her feeling alone and vulnerable, she passed a sporto store. Whenever she saw the window display with the blank-faced male mannequins in running clothes, her pulse surged.

"They should take those mannequins down," she announced to the break room. "At least until this is all over."

When the other women turned to her, brows scrunched, she realized her mistake: she'd spoken about the mannequins as though her coworkers had been privy to her thoughts. She was pretty sure they included her in these conversations only because she was a woman, and therefore a prospective victim of the slapper, even as they suspected she was somehow not quite on their side.

When Margot called Louise to tell her about the slapper, her sister advised her to spend more time at the public library. "All those things he doesn't know," she said, after Margot asked why this asshole would show any respect for the public library. "I bet he finds libraries very intimidating."

Margot was standing in her tiny backyard, struggling to remember the last time she got a decent night's sleep. "Don't you ever want vigilante justice?"

"Vigilante justice is rarely as satisfying as people think. *Auribus teneo lupum* and all that."

Louise paused and then added, "The last bit was Latin."

"I gathered," Margot said, and then told her sister that she needed to go.

She hadn't asked her sister to explain the Latin because that was where Louise was most at home, explaining complicated and arcane things to other people. When she looked up a translation online, she remembered that Louise had answered with the very same phrase when her twin daughters were newborns and Margot had asked how motherhood was going. *I hold a wolf by the ears.* She'd understood the phrase to mean something along the lines of—there is no easy way out.

∎ ∎ ∎

Margot falls asleep with the balcony door open, to the sound of dogs barking and motorbikes stalking the night, and wakes at noon to find the hotel wrapped in the densest fog she's ever seen. She can't make out the hillsides or the sea and the land has been overtaken by a terrible buzzing. Through the glass panes of the balcony door, she watches the wind blow the fog around like smoke. The road race has begun.

She tries Louise again. Her voicemail is full. *Five minutes away from calling Sam*, she texts, and then phones her bank's twenty-four-hour helpline. According to customer service, there is nothing to do but cancel her ATM card and have a new one mailed to her in Minneapolis.

It's early in Boston. Her sister's husband, Sam, has moved into his own apartment in Cambridge, near the river. Her nieces like the place because he has rooftop access. They can watch the rowers practice; they can see the Prudential. Sam is a trained historian who has never finished a book. He hails from New England money and is the kind of person who looks good in gym clothes. Margot suspects Sam has never understood her chronic unease, her relationship to difficulty—he who can drink all night with louche grace and never wind up sobbing at the dinner table or vomiting in the guest bed. He who thinks changing your life is as simple as, well, changing your life.

He doesn't answer and to his voicemail she begins articulating a plan that she has not, in any way, rehearsed. She says that Louise is missing and she is going to Rome to find her. She mentions a friend of Louise's who lives in Monti; she tells Sam this friend has offered to help and so at this stage she does not require anything from him, nothing at all. She is just doing him the courtesy of letting him know that his wife has gone missing in a foreign country and that the whole situation will soon be under control. As she talks, she imagines tracking her sister through grand Roman piazzas, down winding streets, and over stately bridges. She longs to feel capable.

The friend in Monti is real. Margot remembers this person from Sam and Louise's wedding, a decade ago—a tall woman with heavy eyebrows and an emerald brooch pinned to her black dress. Oh, Margot thinks. What was her name?

She opens the balcony door, to let in some air. The hillsides are white and shapeless in the fog, the roads still buzzing. A siren breaks through the race cars and then a powerful wind slams the door shut. She surveys the clothes strewn around her room. The bra splashed across the tile floor, the sandal at rest on the nightstand.

"Today I'll go to Rome," she says before hanging up. "I'm nearly packed."

■ ■ ■

"I'm afraid your passport has been misplaced," Filippo tells her in the lobby, after she informs him that she'll soon be checking out. He appears to be wearing the exact same clothes as yesterday. The red collar of his polo is crinkled, the back tail untucked.

"It doesn't matter," he adds.

"It doesn't matter that you lost my passport?" Margot is incredulous.

"You can't leave today." He points at the road race sign.

"I'm taking the cable car."

"The funicular is closed, due to high winds and fog."

"I think I'd like to speak to a manager," she says.

"Why! I *am* the manager." Filippo claps and laughs, as though she's just told a very funny joke.

Nothing she is saying seems to be imparting a sense of urgency.

"My sister is missing," she tries. "My sister has gone missing in Rome."

Filippo frowns. "You told me she was delayed."

"That was before I knew she was missing!"

"Did you hear that one of the cars went over a cliff?" Filippo rubs the face of his silver watch. "The car was demolished, of course. The driver was thrown through the windshield and landed in the arms of a tree. He broke seventeen bones but stands an excellent chance at staying alive."

"My sister's husband just left her." Margot feels like getting on her knees. She feels like a stiff drink. "She could be having a nervous breakdown. She could be suicidal."

"A miracle," Filippo says, smiling.

■ ■ ■

That afternoon, Margot rushes out into the sloped streets, the cobblestones slick with condensation. She wants to see for herself that the funicular is closed. In the village center, she smells ginger and almond before she spots the bakery sign. She peers in the window and discovers an elaborate display of marzipan: ducklings, baskets of pears, round red apples. The centerpiece is a marzipan lamb, remarkably lifelike and reclining on a bed of fake grass.

She crosses the village, passes through a tall iron gate, and takes a dusty path down to the funicular station: shuttered, just as Filippo said it would be. She watches empty black cars bounce on a still cable; even from the cliffside the roaring race drowns out all other sound. In the distance, she notices a red blossoming in the hillsides, almost like a chain of explosions; the wind ferries over the scent of smoke. Something is on fire.

She climbs back up to the central piazza, with the card-swallowing bankomat and the marzipan-crazed bakery, and follows the sound of the engines down a hooked street, past young men in black aprons offering menus outside vacant restaurants, even though it's late in the day for lunch. At the base of the village, a flat stretch of asphalt has been transformed into a parking lot for Italian race cars. Large black numbers are pasted across the passenger doors. Men in satiny racing costumes lounge by their cars, or stand together in small clusters, talking and smoking cigarettes. Some of the cars are so small it's hard to imagine a grown man folding his body inside. Margot sits on the edge of a low stone wall. The fog is gossamer-thin down here, and she feels exposed.

The wind lifts a red scarf from one driver's neck, a man with a small paunch and a silver beard, and sends it down the road; he chases after it, hands outstretched, a bit awkward in his racing costume. A man in street clothes bends down and intercepts the scarf. He holds on to the scarf for a moment before returning it to the driver and then, perhaps as a gesture of gratitude, the driver gives this man a tour of his car. He lets him sit in the driver's seat. He shows what's under the hood.

It takes Margot several minutes to realize that she's watching the man from the foundation, the man who mistook her for her sister in the corridor and pinned her to the wall, who never let go of that white linen napkin. She watches him grip the car's small black wheel. She watches him crawl out and shake the driver's hand. He looks around and around, surveying the landscape, and then his attention snaps back in her direction and sticks. She stands slowly from the wall, her palms scraping the stone, and the moment she rises, the moment her knees straighten and her lungs expand, he dashes away into the fog and she chases after him.

She scurries up a stone walkway, her back to the racing cars. The path is very steep; it is leading her to something. Through the gusting fog she sees the man slip into a squat marble castle. The structure resembles a chess piece, a rook. Margot shoves open a glass door and flies past a woman in black jeans and a white T-shirt, holding out a brochure for a tour.

"Venus bathed in milk," the woman calls out. "I can show you where."

Margot leaps up a short flight of steps and into a courtyard, the soil lumpy with rock. At first she thinks she's stumbled into an ancient graveyard, with all the stone fragments, some marbled with orange lichen, jutting from the earth— and in a way she's not wrong, given that the courtyard is filled with ruins. Just ahead she spots the man weaving through the fog. She has no idea what she will do when she reaches him, what she will say.

She corners him by a well, marked by a shallow impression in the earth.

"Who *are* you?" He's wearing slacks and a houndstooth sports coat. He grabs himself by the lapels. "What have you done with Louise?"

"Who *am* I?" Margot says, her heart aflame. Her mind flashes back to those faceless mannequins in the sports store window and to Emma dutifully practicing her choke holds and palm strikes, nurtured by the belief that preparation could save her.

Her left arm swings away from her body, as though possessed, and then she feels the base of her palm crash against his nose.

A sound like tires over gravel.

She has no technique, nothing but brute rage on her side; the pain is sudden and immense, a flaming band around her wrist.

The man stumbles forward, toward Margot, as though he might faint into her arms. Blood gushes from one of his nostrils. His lips are coated in it. He brings a hand close to his face and then his fingers flutter away.

"I'm Louise's sister," she says, even more unsure of what to do now.

"My god," says the man.

Right then the woman in the white T-shirt and black jeans comes running into the courtyard, waving a brochure and saying they owe fifteen euros for visiting the ruins, doesn't matter if they took the tour or not.

"Something has happened." The man touches his cheekbone and winces. He spits blood onto the ancient soil.

"Fifteen euros." The woman points a brochure at him, then marches back inside.

"I don't have any money," Margot says. "The bankomat ate my card."

He stares at her for what feels like a long time, the blood slowing to a trickle, and then takes out his wallet. She roots around in her purse and hands him a napkin. He twists the paper into a cone and pushes it up his nostril. Perhaps it is this exchange, reciprocal in nature, that makes it possible for them to leave the castle together and walk back into the village center, in total silence, that is until he turns to her and asks if he can buy her a meal, a drink.

■   ■   ■

Margot has always wanted to be the kind of person who can become too distraught to eat, but the truth is funerals make her hungry. They pick the first restaurant they come upon. By then it's early evening, although the fog makes it feel later. There's a cover for sitting outside, in the chill, so they take an unsteady table in an empty grotto. He sits with his back to the wall, the paper tail of the cone dangling from his nostril, blood crusted to his upper lip. The waiter lingers on his face while delivering menus, then returns with a thin stack of paper napkins and a glass filled with ice. The man glances down at the glinting cubes, but does not make a move.

"Don't you want to clean up?" Margot asks.

"Not particularly," he replies, and she gets it: he wants to make her look at the damage. In the well-lit restaurant she detects new details—the dawn of a receding hairline, the high arch of his eyebrows, twin bridges. Something about his eyes, deep-set and arctic blue, and the stubble darkening his cheeks gives him the look of a person who is exhausted in a way that sleep will not cure.

She goes to the bathroom and splashes cold water on her face. She hears birds chirping. She looks all around, thinking a bird has flown into the bathroom and gotten trapped, only to realize the restaurant is piping birdsong through the walls.

When she returns, the man is finishing a martini. Margot remembers his glazed eyes when he accosted her at the foundation and it is something like comfort, to sit with another drinker right now, to not have to pretend to be different or better.

She asks for a martini too and the least expensive pasta dish, one with tomato and mint, forgetting that he's already offered to pay. The man orders another drink and the veal.

"You were impersonating Louise," he says. "Do you have plans to blackmail me?"

"It was only a name tag."

If she had cried out her right name, what would have happened? Would he have straightened her underwear, lowered her dress? She isn't so sure. She finishes her martini and orders another.

"Where is Louise?" he says next.

"Gone," Margot says. "Missing."

Their food arrives. She eats a bite of pasta, cooked in a broth that tastes beautifully of seawater. She wants to drink from the bowl. She decides she will treat this meal as an interrogation, root out whatever he knows about Louise. She will take all the information she wants and offer nothing in return.

"She's gone missing and I have to find her." Margot pauses. "What can you tell me about my sister?"

He raises his fork, a clump of veal stuck to the tines. "We fuck."

"Did you meet at a conference?" She takes a drink, holds the cold in her mouth.

"What else are conferences for?" A blade of accusation in his voice, as though anyone who attends a conference event should be prepared for whatever happens there.

"I think she might be in Rome," Margot says. "Do you know anything about Rome?"

"Do I know anything about *Rome*?"

"She has an old friend in Monti, or she used to. If only I could remember a name."

"I'm afraid Louise and I don't spend much time in conversation." They've both emptied their cocktail glasses, leaving behind a twist of lemon, a cool shimmer; he orders a carafe of wine.

"Are you a physicist?" she asks.

"Berkeley." He fishes an ice cube from the glass and presses it gingerly to his nose. "You?"

Margot explains about the environmental nonprofit.

"Aha," he says. "A do-gooder."

"It's a paycheck." Already she's too buzzed to be completely dishonest. "The Earth is dying and we are too late to save it."

"An optimist too, I see. Maybe you should teach self-defense lessons instead."

She remarks that there might be a market for such lessons in Minneapolis, given that all summer they were menaced by a man running around and slapping women in the face.

The man opens his hand and a sliver of ice slides down his palm. He hunches over in his chair, hangs his head. His shoulders tremble inside his houndstooth coat. At first she thinks he's crying and is alarmed, ashamed—but no, he's laughing.

"It took a long time for the police to catch him." Under the table she feels her fingers curl into her palms. She feels her voice get big. She imagines her words shaking the laughter right out of him. "You could never let your guard down. Not for one moment."

He looks up. His eyes have that sheen again. The grotto is still empty, no sign of their waiter even, though Margot can hear activity in the kitchen, the hiss of steam, the clank of metal.

"You got slapped," he says. "So you slapped me."

"I never got slapped," she says. "Leave Minneapolis out of this."

"Then what possessed you?" He used the lip of his glass to gesture at his bruised face.

"You know what." She hadn't protested in the shadowed

hallway—that was true. She had felt overwhelmed by the sheer gravitational pull of the moment: the weight of his body pressed against hers, the slur of *Louise* in his wet mouth, her failure to find the words to explain that she had taken her sister's name for the night, even though the explanation was, in hindsight, quite simple. She had just wanted a warm room and a few free drinks and a little revenge on Louise for leaving her alone out here; she hadn't considered what playing the role of her sister would require of her and hadn't that been her first mistake, to not imagine the twisted and dangerous side paths she might find herself on should she veer off course. At the same time, she knew she was lucky that something like this hadn't happened sooner, given the nights she had stumbled through, scarcely aware that she was still on planet Earth. She looked at the man sitting across from her and wondered when he had last felt the euphoria of having been spared.

He picks up the carafe and slops more wine into his glass. "Do I?"

"Why else would you run away from me?" Margot knows he's trying to derail her, to throw her onto a different scent. She begs herself to not fall for it.

"So what will you tell your sister? You can't possibly be planning on the truth."

"What will *you* tell her? That you couldn't see the difference between her and another woman? That you didn't want to?"

"Like I said, we aren't big on small talk."

"Well," she says. "I can't tell her anything until I find her."

He slurps his wine, narrows his arctic eyes. "You want your sister's life. Is that it?"

She shakes her head. "No."

He pounds his fist on the table. "Why else would you impersonate her!"

It's true what she's saying, that she has never desired Louise's life. All she wants is to feel like she isn't being destroyed by the world, even as she doubts she has any right to feel destroyed at all—she has a job and a place to live and she hasn't even been slapped! She's long believed her sister, her brilliant and effortless Louise, figured out the trick—and it's only now, sitting in this damp grotto across from Louise's bloodied lover, that Margot is awakening to the depths of her wrongness, to how much she has missed.

There is no telling where Louise is right now and she can see this man has no intention of helping her.

She stands, her chair clattering, and in the bathroom she vomits into the toilet, to the sound of artificial birdsong. In the grotto, she finds that the bill has been paid in full, as promised, and that the man is gone, his white napkin slung over the back of his chair.

■ ■ ■

Outside Margot is unsteady on her feet. Night has fallen; the goldish eyes of the streetlamps are pressed against the smoky fog. She can no longer hear the racing cars. At long last, silence. She feels something silky brush against her fingertips. The tall white dog trots past, pace brisk, ears alert—as though he is hurrying to keep an appointment.

Her mind feels mercifully blank, her muscles loose.

She wanders the village, gets lost in a tangle of dark, narrow streets, has a few more drinks in a restaurant, this one crowded with drivers in their satin racing costumes. She is heading back in the direction of the hotel when she sees a familiar man cross the central piazza and slip into the bakery, even though the sign on the door reads CHIUSO. Through the window she observes Filippo handing a leather envelope to a young woman in an orange faux fur jacket that swallows up her shoulders. Margot squints at the envelope, large and purse-like, and feels a clutching in her stomach. Yet when the young woman unzips the envelope she pulls out not a passport, but a thin sheet of paper. She disappears into the back and returns carrying what looks to be an enormous cake on a white cardboard sheet, covered in a red gingham cloth. Filippo peeks under the cloth as he talks to her, his free hand rising and falling like an orchestra conductor's, though Margot can't make out his words.

She takes a seat at a wrought-iron café table in the piazza and waits. The café itself is closed, the table lit by a single streetlight.

When Filippo steps outside, holding the cake, he pauses and looks both ways, like he's preparing to navigate a busy street. Margot calls his name, her voice cutting through the darkness and fog. He crosses the piazza and carefully sets the cake down on the café table.

"Oh." His face is pinched with disappointment. "It's you."

"Were you expecting someone else?"

He lights a cigarette and exhales skyward, looking even more tired than he had at the hotel. The single streetlamp illuminates one side of his body, leaves the other in shadow.

"What do you have here?" Margot imagines sinking her hands into a soft, sweet cake. She imagines giving herself, and then Filippo, a mustache made of icing.

Filippo lifts the gingham cloth and she sees that the cake is not a cake at all; rather it is a giant marzipan lamb, rendered in extraordinary detail: the white curls of fur, the seashell-pink color of the inner ears.

"Next week the hotel is hosting a wedding reception." He flicks his cigarette into a thicket of shadow. He sits down. "The bride will want to inspect the marzipan."

In the piazza, her head swimming as it is, the future feels like a fiction, a point on the continuum that's been bundled in fog and pushed out to sea.

"I have to go to Rome," she tells him. "I have to find my sister."

"The race is over," Filippo says. "I'll call you a taxi in the morning myself."

"I can't go anywhere without my passport." She has no idea where the closest U.S. embassy is located. Trapani? Palermo? "Did you take it? Are you going to give it back?"

"I suppose you'll find out tomorrow." He unclips the silver watch and places it on the table. He shakes out his wrist. "Do you people ever consider the possibility that none of you have anything that we want?"

She stares down at the lamb's polished hooves and silvered snout, its round white belly. The longer she looks the more bloated the belly seems, so pink and swollen that if she found a knife and cut it open something alive would tumble out.

"This looks very real." With her fingernail she taps a marzipan hoof.

He tells her it is not enough for the lamb to look real—it must look at once like a real lamb and like something sprung from a dream. It must have a certain aura. That was what separated the marzipan amateurs from the masters, the ability to create the right aura.

"An aura," Margot repeats. Once a coworker at the non-profit told her that she had an unsettled aura about her. She closes her eyes and is visited by a disembodied hand holding a white linen napkin. The hand shakes the napkin like a matador luring a bull.

Her eyes snap open. She sniffs the air and catches a hint of smoke.

"The hillsides are on fire," she says.

"The firefighters only get paid if there are fires." Filippo pulls the gingham cloth over the lamb. "So they start the fires and then run around putting them out."

She hears a rushing sound and then the white dog gallops across the piazza, leading a pack of a dozen—no, two dozen, three dozen—strays. She watches the leader fling its massive paws into the night, white fur rigid as armor. Some dogs run in a long canter, others in a chop. They make her want to get down on all fours. They make her want to go fast and far. How do she and Filippo know that they are not just living inside a dog's dream?

"Louise," Filippo says.

She clutches the iron arms of her chair. It is a terrible shock, that name. She remembers walking through the automatic doors of the hotel, feeling jet-lagged and bewildered by her sister's garbled call. She remembers setting her suitcase down at the front desk and saying *Louise*.

She looks down at the silver watch on the table, the hands clocking the changing hour. It is nearly midnight.

Through the cloth she strokes the marzipan lamb's fat belly. "My name is Margot."

"Margot?" He frowns. "Who's Margot?"

When it happens she thinks, *For as long as I live I'll never forget this sound.*

In the village, all the church bells begin to ring.

In the hillsides, the dogs howl.

ACKNOWLEDGMENTS

I'm wildly and eternally grateful to the magazines that first published these stories and the editors who worked hard to make them better: Emily Nemens at *The Paris Review*; Paul Reyes and Allison Wright at the *Virginia Quarterly Review*; David Lynn and Caitlin Horrocks at the *Kenyon Review*; Lincoln Michel and Nadxieli Nieto for *Tiny Crimes: Very Short Tales of Mystery and Murder*; Nicole Chung at *Catapult*; Libby Flores and Andrew Bourne at *BOMB*; Claire Boyle at *McSweeney's*; Halimah Marcus at *Electric Literature*; and Molly Elizalde at *Lenny Letter*.

I am enormously indebted to the Civitella Ranieri Foundation for the magical time in Umbertide, where some of these stories were written. Special thanks to Dana, Ilaria, Diego, and to my kind and brilliant cohort of artists. I'm grateful as well to the Writers' Room of Boston for space and to the New York Public Library and *American Short Fiction* for encouragement along the way. And thank you to my Boston fight fam—I have never been so happy to spend time with people who are trying to punch me in the face.

Thank you to my early readers—Elliott, Lauren, Jami, R.O., Mike, and Josh. I would still be at sea without you.

I am grateful daily to have found a home at FSG. Bottomless thanks to Chloe Texier-Rose and to Jackson Howard for all that you do. Thanks also to Na Kim for the killer cover, and to Debra Helfand, Rebecca Caine, and Frieda Duggan. At Curtis Brown, thank you to Holly Frederick, Maddie Tavis, Sarah Gerton, and Jazmina Young.

Emily Bell and Katherine Fausset—I am the luckiest to get to work with you. Thank you for everything, on the page and off.

My family—I have never been more grateful for you.

Mom—thank you for being there.

Marigold—welcome to the world, babe. You are giving us all hope.

Dad—I miss you every day. Thank you for believing that I could write stories.

Paul—you are my heart and you make everything possible. Thank you into infinity.

A Note About the Author

Laura van den Berg is the author of the story collections *What the World Will Look Like When All the Water Leaves Us* and *The Isle of Youth*, and the novels *Find Me* and *The Third Hotel*, the latter of which was a finalist for the New York Public Library Young Lions Fiction Award and an Indie Next pick, and was named a best book of 2018 by more than a dozen publications. She is the recipient of a Rosenthal Family Foundation Award from the American Academy of Arts and Letters, the Bard Fiction Prize, a PEN/O. Henry Award, and a MacDowell Colony fellowship, and is a two-time finalist for the Frank O'Connor International Short Story Award. Born and raised in Florida, she splits her time between the Boston area and central Florida with her husband and dog.